NORTHFIELD BRANCH
(847) 446-5990

D0287599

SEPTEMBER
2023

Winnetka-Northfield Public
Library District
Winnetka, IL 60093
(847) 446-7220

MELISSA DE LA CRUZ

DISNEP • HYPERION

LOS ANGELES   NEW YORK

Copyright © 2023 by Melissa de la Cruz

All rights reserved. Published by Disney • Hyperion, an imprint
of Buena Vista Books, Inc. No part of this book may be reproduced
or transmitted in any form or by any means, electronic or mechanical,
including photocopying, recording, or by any information storage and
retrieval system, without written permission from the publisher.
For information address Disney • Hyperion, 125 West End Avenue,
New York, New York 10023.

First Edition, September 2023
10 9 8 7 6 5 4 3 2 1
FAC-004510-23194
Printed in the United States of America

This book is set in Adobe Caslon Pro/Monotype
Designed by Marci Senders
Illustrations created in Adobe Photoshop

Library of Congress Control Number for Hardcover Edition: 2023931917
ISBN 978-1-368-08374-4

Reinforced binding

Visit www.DisneyBooks.com

SUSTAINABLE FORESTRY INITIATIVE ® Certified Sourcing
www.forests.org
SFI-01681

Logo Applies to Text Stock Only

For my duo: Mike and Mattie, always

Prologue

THE WAITING ROOM

Once upon a time, not very long ago—in fact, it might have happened just last month or last week, or maybe, just maybe, it's happening right now—eight very different students from across the country sit quietly in a holding room, sizzling with anticipation.

They are confused. Anxious. Sweaty.

No one knows what's going on or what's going to happen next. This is not exactly what they envisioned the Octagon Valley Institute's three-day conference would entail. And that's really saying something. After all, these are the most advanced middle schoolers in the country—they're blessed with huge imaginations. It's just that their daydreams of this weekend didn't include being trapped in a waiting room for a seemingly endless amount of time.

How long has it been?

Long.

You see, my friends, the thing is, before arriving at the Institute, each of them had dreamed about what this three-day summit would be like, what it would bring into their lives, what kinds of opportunities and knowledge and secrets of the universe it would unlock.

Does that last part seem far-fetched? Well, let's not get ahead of ourselves.

Point is, these eight middle schoolers (seven really, but that's another thing we'll get to later, *Harold*) are quite astute. They have minds that can expertly calculate a multitude of conclusions and predictions. Right now, however, as they sit waiting on uncomfortable chairs at variously shaped desks in a small, otherwise empty room, not one of them is able to imagine what comes next.

Edwin Edgefield, an eleven-year-old Black boy, small for his age, young for his grade, had hoped that the three-day weekend would involve some rousing debate over which multiverse theory was most accurate, and at least a few games of chess. These kids are supposed to be his peers, aren't they? He might finally have some stimulating discussion and competition in his life. A boy can hope! So here he is. Waiting for his educational adventure to officially begin.

"Uh, are we supposed to take the blindfolds off now?" one of the girls says.

The other kids start talking. Edwin feels exposed. Did

they all take their blindfolds off? No one told them to take their blindfolds off. Would taking it off mean breaking the rules?

"Anyone else feel like it was weird that we had to be blindfolded to get here?" another girl's voice asks. "What was that about? I wanted to see the corridors!"

"I'm sure Onasander had his reasons," Edwin replies.

"You're really obsessed with him, aren't you?" the girl asks judgmentally. "Why are you still blindfolded?"

Edwin pulls off his blindfold and blinks. It's Maureen Pearson. She's the one staring him down. "Aren't we all obsessed with him?" he asks.

"Not really," Maureen says. "I mean, obviously he's super famous. Being associated with him gives us clout." She tosses her hair over her shoulder and walks away.

"If that's what matters to you," Edwin replies.

He looks around at the other kids in the room.

A white boy with a buzz cut and sour expression whom we shall call Anton Chesky, because that is his name, waited for a maximum of ten seconds after the door closed to whip off his blindfold and whip *out* a portable gaming console, which he is now playing. A Filipino girl who took elaborate notes at the parent drop-off, Anabelle "Ting-Ting" Costanza, is now reviewing these notes studiously, though we can't imagine what she could have possibly written down. *Hello? Greetings, Octos? Welcome to the Valley?*

Two other white kids, Harold Postman Jr. VIII (yes,

the eighth Harold Junior, you read that right) and Maureen, both of whom look like they stepped right out of a teen soap opera set on the Upper East Side of New York (which is actually where Maureen is from), are huddled together, whispering and snickering at the others. The California kids—Eun-Kyung "Li'l Kimmy" Kim, a Korean girl, and an Indian boy named Dilip Aggarwal—are, meanwhile, leaning back on their chairs with their feet kicked up on a desk to show off Nike Dunks (Li'l Kimmy) and Air Jordans (Dilip). Last but not least, there's Julie Carter, a red-haired white girl who's tapping her fingers in a captivating rhythm on her desk as if composing a masterpiece in her head.

So Edwin was the last to remove his blindfold. For some reason, this makes him blush.

The small, stuffy waiting room is filled with this crackling, anticipatory energy. They can't wait to get started! But what are they waiting for, exactly? Are they in competition with one another? Ting-Ting, the notes-taker, and the snooty kids, Harold and Maureen, certainly seem to think so.

But aren't they all here as a reward for being the only kids who passed the Octagon Valley Assessment for the Extra-Ordinary? Only eight of them in the whole country did. Then why would they be in a competition now? Isn't the competition over?

"So, when do you guys think someone's going to come get us?" Dilip asks, leaning so far back on his chair that it seems to almost hover and is in obvious danger of tipping over.

Suddenly, they hear a loud clicking noise.

Eight heads whip around to the door in the back of the room. Eight hearts sink at the sound. They are the smartest middle schoolers in America. They know what just happened.

Ting-Ting runs to the door and tries the handle. "It's locked!" she cries, even though they all already know that. They didn't earn the highest scores on the Octagon Valley Assessment for nothing.

Meanwhile, mechanical bars are slowly lowering over the small windows of the small room.

"What's going on?" Julie asks in a quiet voice.

"Why is it so hot all of a sudden . . . ?" Dilip notes, fanning himself with his T-shirt collar.

"Are we trapped?!" Maureen shrieks. "Of course we are. I should have *known*. . . ."

"Trapped? This is unacceptable!" Harold says, sounding a lot like the CEO of a multi-bazillion-dollar company, and more specifically, just like his father, Harold Jr. VII, whose two favorite phrases are *This is unacceptable!* and *Fire up the jet!* In a voice that booms across the tiny room, Harold declares, "My father will be hearing about this!"

One senses that Harold likes to comfort himself with the thought that his father would care that his son is trapped in a very small room that's slowly losing oxygen, but that this comfort is a total fantasy. If Harold Jr. VII did hear about this, he would most likely tell his secretary he'll get to it later, after the many more important matters on his desk.

Edwin ignores the panic all around him and feels a tingle on his skin, the kind he gets whenever something big is about to happen.

Sure enough, and soon enough, the sound of static fills the room, and then a smooth voice purrs though the overhead speakers.

"Hello again, Octos."

It's a voice they've heard so many times before. A voice they've heard on news reports and on television, a voice from *Octo Talks* on their laptops late at night. On their phones, on podcasts, on their streaming services. A voice they'd heard mere moments ago, during The Welcome, Etc., when they'd first arrived at the Octagon Valley Institute and been congratulated for their terrific, weekend-winning performances on the Octagon Valley Assessment.

The voice of the one and only Onasander Octagon. The visionary. The smartest and most mysterious man in the world. Their idol. Their mentor (they hoped). But that was before they were brought to this room. That was before they were *locked* in this room.

"Welcome to the *real* Octagon Valley Institute," Onasander drawls.

The way he says *real* would make your skin crawl if you were there.

And with that, the lights go out, and the room plunges into darkness and screaming.

So much screaming.

(And none of it for ice cream.)

PART ONE:

THE OCTAGON VALLEY ASSESSMENT

FOR THE EXTRA-ordinary

Chapter One

THE OVAEO

Well now, let's leave those eight kids behind and take it back a few steps *before* we plunged into utter darkness and terrified screaming, shall we? Give you a bit of background before we discover what happens to our eight (or seven—are we counting Harold? *Should* we count Harold? Okay, *fine*, let's say eight for now, since he's still in the story. Hmpf.) brilliant middle schoolers.

After all, what's a story without a backstory?

Let's rewind!

The first thing you should know is that this year, for the first time, all across this great, grand country of ours, budding young minds were put to the test. Oh, yes, yes, budding young minds are *always* being put to the test—so many tests! ERBs and ISEEs and PSATs and SATs and

EKGs and MRIs. Oh, the last two aren't the same sort of test.

Anyhoo!

This was a *very* special test.

A new test.

But hold on now, it's not *actually* a test—we don't have those anymore, what are you, living in 1985? We don't have tests anymore in this country! Just like we don't have bullies. Nope! We don't say the *b* word. Because if we don't call them bullies, how can they, um, bully? So yeah, no bullies, no tests. Nope! What we have these days are *Unfortunate Incidents that Hopefully Do Not Warrant a Lawsuit Against the School* and *assessments*.

We have *assessments*. After all, you can't fail an assessment, right? You're just being . . . assessed. Analyzed. There are no right or wrong answers. This is just an evaluation of skills, should you have any. And if you don't have, um, skills or, um, brains—move along, move along, nothing to see here. Nothing to worry about! No one's failed! No one's deemed lesser! No one's a loser! Because no one's a winner either!

TROPHIES FOR ALL!

Ahem.

Anyhoo . . .

So this new thing that every middle schooler across the country had to take is called the OVAEO. (Try saying that super-fast and backward! Not to be confused with EVOO, or

Extra Virgin Olive Oil!) The OVAEO is not something you put on pizza and salads, it is the Octagon Valley Assessment for the Extra-Ordinary, which was created by the incredibly mysterious and blindingly brilliant Onasander Octagon of the Octagon Valley Institute.

There had been almost no information about what the Octagon Valley Assessment for the Extra-Ordinary would be about, only that every school in the country, from the fanciest private schools to the most poorly funded public schools, would be administering the test to their students. And this was not just another boring math quiz doled out by their homeroom teacher, nor a statewide punch card to determine whether the school would have enough markers for its whiteboards next year.

Nope!

Onasander Octagon announced that he was searching for the country's best and brightest, the next generation of Extra-Ordinary kids who would become tomorrow's leaders. For those who dream of becoming astronauts or exploring the mysteries of the oceans, of cracking ancient codes or cataloging the known and unknown phenomena of the universe, for those who dream big and wide and want to swallow up the whole world, the OVAEO (again, not an olive oil) was a beacon of potential and opportunity.

It was an assessment to uncover the cream of the crop, the less-than-one-percent, the trailblazers, the most creative, the most ingenious, those who can, not just those who want to. Those who passed the assessment would be invited for a three-day summit at the Octagon Valley Institute in the mountains of Montana for a series of lectures and workshops where this next generation's stars would meet one another and begin forging their futures.

Unfortunately, we can't all be Extra. And of all the thousands of sixth-graders who took this test, only eight were proven to be Extra-Ordinary. Because to pass the assessment, you not only have to get 99.99999999% of the questions right, you also have to get the *108th* question right.

In truth, it all came down to that one question. The question was: *Do you want ice cream?*

No! That wasn't the 108th question, silly!

The question was:

Are you a yak?

No! That wasn't the 108th question, silly!

The question was:

Do you see this question?

For all intents and purposes, it does not matter one fig (one polygon?) what the question was, because *noticing* that the question *existed* was the first test. Ahem. Assessment.

The first of the eight to answer correctly was Edwin Edgefield. Actually, Edwin wasn't just the first of the eight to get it right, but he was also the very first of all of the sixth-graders all across the country to finish the assessment. Edwin sat in the middle seat in the middle row of his public school classroom in his home state of Tennessee, where his Jamaican grandparents immigrated. He always likes to sit in the middle seat, middle laterally and longitudinally. Everyone in school knows that the seat dead center of the classroom is reserved for Edwin. At first they had made fun of him for this strange and unusual behavior (but they did not bully! No! No bullying!), but eventually, as is human nature, they just got used to it.

Though Edwin may have double the IQ of Albert Einstein (a fact that caused the IQ testers to test him twenty-seven times, just to be sure), there are other things he still hasn't even begun to master. Tying his shoes, for example. Which is why his go-to look is a pair of sneakers with butterfly clips. It's caused some teasing, sure, but what hasn't? His small stature? His owlish gaze? Edwin's always known he's different: Other kids have made that *abundantly* clear to him over the years, even if repeated visits by his mother to the principal's office always ended in the same way—with a revisiting of the school policies that say there isn't any bullying in the school, only unfortunate incidents that hopefully do not warrant a lawsuit against the school.

So, yes, Edwin knows he is not like the other kids.

He is smaller. He is smarter. He cannot tie his shoes.

But does that have to be a bad thing? He doesn't think so. That's what butterfly clips are for!

That's why it didn't surprise him too much when he finished the OVAEO in the blink of an eye. Literally.

His teacher handed out the tests, sat down, yawned, and then there was Edwin, standing with the test in hand, all filled out.

Even the 108th question.

"Can I go to lunch?" he asked. "I'm hungry."

Chapter Two

ON THE WAY TO OCTAGON VALLEY

"Don't freak out," Edwina says, glancing at Edwin. "Yes, we're almost there."

Tower spires. That's what Edwin can see. Emerging from the forest, on the side of a mountain, sticking out above the massively tall trees, are colorful tops of turrets like something out of a medieval fairy tale. The Octagon Valley Institute. He's never seen anything like it outside of picture books.

"I'm not freaking out," Edwin says to his mother, Edwina, from the passenger seat.

"You're doing the knee thing," she says.

"I am?"

Edwin looks down and sees his knee bouncing urgently. His nervous habit. His mother usually gets him to stop by placing one of his heftier books on his knee (which calms him with its weight and distracts him with its contents), but since she's driving, he's left to his own devices. Which is probably good, since he'll be left to his own devices soon anyway. For three days, at least. And Edwin feels like anything could happen in the next three days. There's a reason why everyone always says that what happens at Octagon Valley stays at Octagon Valley. Or is that Las Vegas? That city has a lot to answer for, including this clichéd phrase.

Edwina tosses her phone into Edwin's lap so he can pick new music. He decides on an ambient lo-fi playlist. He listens to this while studying, one of his most calming pastimes. Yes, Edwin studies *for fun.*

"There's no need to be nervous, Edwin. You've already aced the assessment. This"—she motions around them to the mountains in the distance, the snack bags in the back seat, the sun shining on the trees on the other side of the windshield—"this is the payoff!" She reaches over to rub Edwin's shoulder soothingly.

"You're right, you're right." He nods.

He does the breathing exercise that she taught him to calm down the nervous system. Breathe in for four counts, hold for four counts, breathe out for four counts, hold for four counts.

"I know you feel like there are huge expectations on you right now, that this weekend is what you've been working toward for so long," Edwina says. "But just remember that you've only been working toward this because you want to. This is something *you* want. It's a great opportunity, but it's supposed to be fun. You need to take some pressure off yourself."

Easier said than done. When the test was announced, Edwin practically exploded from excitement. He saw it on his phone, up in his bedroom, while his mom saw it on the news downstairs. As soon as the words had registered in their minds, they flew out of their seats, running to each other, colliding in squeals and hugs on the stairs.

The words that flashed on their screens: *Onasander Octagon Announces the Octagon Valley Assessment for the Extra-Ordinary.* Who could have ever thought something like this would happen? That Onasander Octagon, the myste-rious genius running the Octagon Valley Institute, would announce a test for sixth-graders all around the country? The very year that Edwin is in the sixth grade! *The Octagon Valley Assessment for the Extra-Ordinary.* Those were the words on everyone's lips after it was announced. The name appeared in the headlines of newspapers, on news tickers, and it was trending everywhere on social media.

Everyone needed to know: What exactly was it? And what did Extra-Ordinary mean, precisely? But, in typical Onasander fashion, he stayed silent. The only detail that anyone knew—if something this massively huge could be called a detail—was that the prize for passing the test was a weekend at the Octagon Valley Institute. What the weekend would entail exactly was uncertain. But Onasander also mentioned in the announcement that if things went well over the weekend for the winners, this potential "next generation" of Extra-Ordinary minds would get summer internships at the Octagon Valley Institute once they were in high school and would even be offered a job at the Institute after college graduation. Edwin and Edwina didn't even need to talk about it. It was obvious. Edwin would pass the assessment; he would do anything he had to do to be one of the chosen few. The Extra-Ordinary.

"Three whole days," Edwin says as the spires in the distance grow closer. "What will we do for three whole days?"

"They mentioned lectures and workshops in the letter, didn't they?" Edwina asks.

"Yeah, but they didn't send a precise schedule." Edwin frowns. "You'd think a guy like Onasander Octagon would be more organized."

Edwin knows what everyone in the world knows about Onasander Octagon. But really, that means he knows nothing. Onasander Octagon is an enigma wrapped in a mystery. People often say that Onasander Octagon seems like he is gifted with an endless amount of time, far more than the rest of us. Because how could one man work on so many things? Edwin has surmised that this is partly why, despite barely ever making public appearances, Onasander is, well, famous. How could one man spearhead the invention of a surgery that can save bomb victims, discover a new type of sea creature (a "squigfin," he named it, which looks like a flying squirrel but is blue and has gills), *and* publish a philosophical text about having hope during the climate crisis? In one year? And that's only the top three most reported-on projects. Plus, all the hardcore Double O–heads know that his most interesting and innovative work is never made public and kept completely behind closed doors. What is he working on? A portal to Mars? A time-travel machine? A cure for cancer? No one ever knows until the day it's revealed, to much fanfare and another round of global, fawning applause.

Onasander is largely regarded as a philanthropist, inventor, and cutting-edge scientist. That's the first line of his Wikipedia entry. Edwin has the whole page memorized. Onasander believes in an interdisciplinary approach to research and invention that includes significant value placed on the arts and humanities as well as the sciences. He conducts his research and project development at the Octagon Valley Institute. The place is a modern-day legend. Camelot and the Google Campus rolled into one.

There are countless articles written in every newspaper and magazine in the country about his innovations in the realm of medical research, technological inventions, and philosophical writings and contributions to the arts. But about his personal life? No one knows anything.

No one even knows how old he is. Or where he went to school. Or if he has a family.

Every magazine profile is the same, and Edwin has read them all. Onasander meets the journalist profiling him somewhere impressive but public, like the Metropolitan Museum of Art in New York, or the Sydney Opera House after a performance of an experimental Afro-futurist opera he's funded. He's always wearing some wildly colored suit: mauve, vermilion, daffodil. The journalists always comment on that. His wispy white hair and rotation of statement glasses are familiar to most people these days; he's been on enough magazine covers. But never, ever, ever will Onasander meet a journalist at the Octagon Valley Institute.

No one has ever been to the Octagon Valley Institute. No pictures of it even exist online, which seems impossible to Edwin. But it's the truth. The closest Edwin's ever gotten to seeing it is looking at the blurry aerial shots online, after he eventually found the exact coordinates of the Institute on an obscure internet page. And every time he brings it up on any screen, after staring at the image for a few seconds, trying to decipher the blur, there's a glitch, and Google Earth catapults him somewhere completely different.

When reporters inevitably try to get personal with Onasander, attempting to get the human angle for their articles by asking about his upbringing, his hometown, what his family is like, early influences, the same thing always happens. Onasander shuts down, refusing to answer the questions. He scolds the journalists for playing into what he calls "the American media's fascination with gossip and aimless personal chatter" over the *real* story: his work. Lately, the media has stopped even trying. Edwin guesses that Onasander's probably in his sixties, which means he grew up in a time before everything was so easily and completely documented and available online. In a world of Instagram, TikTok, YouTube, and the dark web, one of Onasander's most impressive feats is his ability to keep his life a mystery.

Onasander's unknown background has only augmented his intrigue. Edwin's certainly done his fair share of internet deep-diving looking for some crumb of a clue as to where Onasander came from. There are whole threads online about it, theories abounding on every platform, endless conspiracy videos. Each posits a different answer as to where Onasander came from and where he got the money to build the Octagon Valley Institute. Is Onasander Octagon an exiled prince? An orphaned runaway who struck crypto gold? The progeny of a dead rock-and-roll legend who left him his fortune? No one seems to know. Those are the tamer bets, but there are far more outlandish ones too. Edwin has his own speculations, but he'd never say them out loud, let alone write about it online.

Students who answered the 108th question correctly were notified by letter. Edwin found it charming, and thrilling, to receive the news this way. After all, what is done by mail anymore? The only mail Edwin has ever received is five dollars in a card from his paternal grandparents on his birthday and Christmas every year, even though his dad died when he was a baby. Edwin's stomach did somersaults when Edwina pulled out the thick cream envelope with the Octagon Valley Institute logo embossed on it: an open palm with the infinity symbol hovering above it. Just looking at the fancy envelope, he knew he had passed the test.

He had been chosen.

Deemed Extra.

As they drive, Edwin has the letter on his lap. He's put it in a protective sleeve. He knew it would get obliterated by his fingerprints otherwise: He couldn't let go of it once he got it. Even now, as they make their way toward the Octagon Institute, he keeps staring at it just to remind himself that this is all real.

In the letter, Onasander congratulated Edwin on passing the assessment, saying he was one of very few kids in the country who did. He implored Edwin and the other recipients not to post the letter on social media and to keep quiet about everything leading up to the weekend summit. Edwin wouldn't dare spread the news. He felt like he held the keys to the city—no, the keys to a mystical, previously uncharted world! He would never betray that trust, though some of the other recipients of the letter wouldn't find it so easy (*ahem*). On the thick, beautiful paper, Onasander hinted vaguely at the workshops and lectures that would be offered during the reward weekend. Edwin studied the words meticulously. There was a surprisingly large chunk of time at the beginning reserved for what was called "The Welcome, Etc." He paused on this, curious, but his eyes were quickly drawn to a description of the botanical gardens where an herbology class would be held.

Edwin gulps as they get closer. It's not that Edwin's terrified of anything in particular. It's more a general, ambient terror. The terror of knowing that for the first time in your life, you might be close to getting something you've dreamed about. You might meet other kids who think like you. Who enjoy the same stuff as you. Who might even become your friends. Edwin has never really had friends. The most he's ever had are slightly-less-than-hostile acquaintances. Which were, at least, better than the bullies.

Not that there are bullies anymore.

But then again, what if these kids don't want to be his friends? How much worse would it be to discover that you've finally found people who share your interests, but they still don't like you? Gosh, that last one has never even occurred to him before now. He's spiraling, he's spiraling! He needs to square-breathe. Breathe in, hold, out, hold. You can do it, Edwin!

Edwin's sure there isn't one smart and ambitious kid in the country who wouldn't want to work for Onasander, and he's right. Onasander has his finger on the pulse of every industry, runs the coolest, most prestigious company and research facility in the world, and is ethical on top of it! Not like those guys who just say they're doing good and then the moment they raise money, they hoover the funds to the Bahamas! Yes, Edwin reads the news!

There's nowhere else like the Octagon Valley Institute when it comes to working on the most exciting, innovative, creative, explorative projects known to humankind. Edwin still can't believe he passed the test. It's like winning a golden ticket to the rest of your life. Plus, Edwin has a strong feeling that Onasander might have some answers to questions that have been on Edwin's mind for a while now.

"So, which part of the weekend are you most excited for?" Edwina asks, interrupting Edwin's train of thought.

"Honestly, I don't even know how to answer that." Edwin imagines what might await him. For once, his mind doesn't go to the worst-case scenario. He imagines friendly discussions about favorite books and documentaries, invigorating sparring matches, swapping answers for difficult equations. Laughter. Camaraderie. He suddenly realizes he's grinning. Maybe this won't be so terrifying after all.

Chapter Three

LI'L PRODIGIES

he day of the OVAEO (not the olive oil!), a shy twelve-year-old girl with bright red hair braided into two long plaits skulked into a Connecticut classroom to fill out the assessment as quickly as she was able so she could get the heck away from her torturous classmates. The entire class was still mad at her for the hacking fiasco, but in her defense, she didn't think she could put a bigger target on her back than the one she already had. Walking into the classroom, she cursed her parents for the millionth time for making her go to middle school to learn "social skills." Who needs social skills when you started playing first violin for the New York Philharmonic when you were three years old? Yeah, you read that right.

Julie Louisa Carter is low-key the twenty-first-century

Mozart. She's even won a Grammy for one of her compositions. But did Mozart have to put up with snot-nosed classmates voting him "Most Annoying" in the fifth-grade yearbook? They probably didn't even have yearbooks in eighteenth-century Vienna. That was smart of them. You might be wondering why "Most Annoying" is even a yearbook category? Well, it's not, but one of Julie's classmates petitioned for a write-in campaign. Exercising your democratic rights never looked so mean.

To add insult to injury, those same cretins toilet-papered her house the night before elementary school graduation. She bet that the last conductor of the New York Philharmonic didn't have their house TP-ed while they were conducting. Though, to be fair, the last conductor was an adult. Four years after Julie started playing in the orchestra, they asked her to be the conductor. She has a special touch. And a special stool so that she can see over the top of the podium.

Julie's not one to take a hit lightly, so there was no way she was letting her classmates get away scot-free with conducting a write-in campaign to vote her "Most Annoying" *and* toilet-papering her house. This girl is shy, but she doesn't suffer fools. And good news for her, it's possible to get revenge in today's world without ever looking your enemy in the eye. So she hit her classmates where it hurts. No, not their stomachs. Their apps. Right as summer break was about to start and her classmates were stretching their fingers in anticipation of endless screen time (every sixth-grader knows how to get past the screen-time "password" that parents put on their phones to limit use), Julie hacked all their accounts and shut them out of all their social media. No *Roblox*, no *Minecraft*, no TikTok, no *Kim Kardashian: Hollywood* (not that anyone still plays that game—does anyone except forty-year-olds even know it exists? *Ahem*). Instagram, Snapchat, Discord? Forget it. Some of them even resorted to using Facebook, just for something to do. Julie left Facebook alone just to torture them.

Which is why, as she skulked into the classroom to fill out the OVAEO, she received a rousing round of boos.

"Boooo!"

"Boooo!"

"It's Julie! Boooo!"

Have you ever been booed to your face? Outside of a basketball or baseball or volleyball game when you were playing for the opposing team and the home team's parents were unsportsmanlike? (Like the *b* word, the *boo* word is out of fashion now. It's against the rules to boo. No boo. Not to be confused with the overpriced sushi restaurant or the planet that Jar Jar Binks calls home.)

Bet you haven't.

Bet you've never been booed.

To your face.

By a bunch of social-media-deprived sixth-graders.

Well, it is not pleasant, let me tell you.

Julie, bless her heart—it's what they say in the South

when they pity you—didn't care, though. She's got loads of DGAH energy—Don't Give a Hoot! (This is going in the Scholastic Book Fair, people, come on!) What does she need friends for? Who even wants friends? She's never had one and never needed one.

She has her music. Her orchestra. Her standing ovations.

So yeah, no social skills. But she has everything else. And more importantly, she has the passwords to all their social media accounts. And she's never giving them back!

PFFFFT!

Boo all you want, she'll just take away your Facebook accounts too! Then what? You'll have to talk to each other face-to-face? As if!

Julie ignored everyone, filled out her OVAEO as quickly as she could manage while still reading all the questions thoroughly, dropped it on the teacher's desk, and left to catch the train to New York for orchestra rehearsal. She had a requiem to run.

Over in the sprawling, not-so-smoggy-anymore city of Los Angeles, Li'l Kimmy was feeling good. She was gonna slay this assessment, she knew that much. She'd been studying like her life depended on it since it was announced. Thank goodness she's a grind, because Onasander has mad connections to the music industry, or at least that's how the rumors go. The dude supposedly knows everyone who's anyone! A dude who knows Princess Nokia, Noname, and Yaeji? That is a good dude to know.

Growing up in Koreatown, Eun-Kyung Kim, aka Li'l Kimmy, has been deeply influenced by the city's music scene. Seriously, do not tell her parents, but she and her cousin Sully have been sneaking out to DIY shows around the city ever since last summer. A whole new world opened up to Eun-Kyung, and that's when she became Li'l Kimmy. She's still having a hard time convincing her classmates to do the name switch, but they'll get used to it. They've come a long way since they used to make fun of her for being too emotional, too sensitive, too volatile.

When her cousin took her to her first concert, and she saw girls like her onstage rapping and dancing, she knew the answer to all her problems. She needed to become chill like them. Cool like them. Confident like them. And ever since she committed to it full throttle, started keeping her emotions in check to keep her cool girl image intact—kids at school have left her alone.

So yeah, some of them still aren't calling her Li'l Kimmy, but wait till they see her face on a billboard, bro! Then they'll really get it and get why she's been mixing GarageBand tracks and dropping SoundCloud links on her Insta like no one's business. Okay, so they haven't gotten that many plays yet. But all the best SoundCloud rappers started out way underground, right?

She's not unsuccessful, just *undiscovered*.

However, she can't spend all her time recording her freestyles. Because not only is she going to become a famous rapper, she's going to become a famous rapper with a PhD. You know that's right! Li'l Kimmy is a next-level brain and her grades are super smooth, yo. This girl works hard to make sure she covers all the bases!

Which was how she noticed the 108th question. She was staring down the OVAEO like she was gonna devour it, and devour it she did. Every last morsel, including the 108th question that every single one of her classmates missed. She didn't let *any* question pass her by on the assessment.

Which is how she finds herself, shortly after handing it in, at the Octagon Valley Institute.

SLAYYYYY!

Chapter Four

WELCOME TO OCTAGON VALLEY

"**Y**ou know," Edwina says as they wind down the Institute's long driveway, "all this is reminding me of when I was pregnant with you."

Edwin sighs, knowing she's trying to distract him from his anxiety. He knows exactly what's coming. His mom loves to tell this story, and he's heard it a thousand times. It keeps her from being too sad that his father died before Edwin was born.

"Other mothers, when they get pregnant, they crave certain things," Edwina continues. "Pickles, ice cream, Hot Cheetos. But when I was pregnant? No. I didn't crave food! I craved chess. Chess! I'd never even *played* chess before I got pregnant with you, and then suddenly there I was, hankering for a game at all hours of the day."

Edwin laughs and closes his eyes. He lets himself get distracted, lost in his origin story, so that he doesn't look at the buildings that hold everything he's ever wanted. It would be a real bummer to start the weekend off with a panic attack.

"So, I started playing chess with everyone around me. It made no sense! I had never even learned to play chess, and there I was, playing with your grandpa, with the neighbors, with all my friends, and not only was I playing, I was *winning*. A friend of mine told his coworker, a professor at the local university, about me and how good I was without ever being taught. He decided to play me, and I won! This man had been studying Russian chess technique for years, and still, I won! No one could understand it, least of all me."

Edwin grins, knowing what's coming next.

"What no one else knew, though, was that it wasn't really me playing. I couldn't tell anyone about it, and I couldn't explain it, but I felt, in my bones, that it was you, my little boy in my belly, telling me what moves to make. You'd tap my stomach in such a way that I just knew where to go."

"I wish I could remember that part!" Edwin chuckles.

"And the professor, he was not happy to have lost. So he set me up against the IBM chess machine Deep Blue. You know, men like that, they so often have trust in machines over people. Isn't that always the case! Anyhow, I certainly played the machine, but I really should say *we* played the machine. And we won! No one could believe it. They even gave me a plaque to commemorate the win. But I told everyone, even though it's my name on the plaque . . ."

"It really should be mine," Edwin finishes, finally opening his eyes.

Edwina smiles at him. "I always knew you were special, Edwin. From then on, I knew you had something different about you. You're not like other kids. You have . . . something extra. Just like your dad. I miss him so. You know what I'm talking about, don't you?"

Edwin thinks he does. He nods.

His eyes now open, he sees how close they are to the Institute. In front of them, there's a massive wrought iron gate with *Octagon Valley Institute* written in swirling text. Edwin's stomach does a flip. Next to the gate is a small booth.

"Oh! Here we are, the security gate, like Onasander's letter said."

Edwina pulls up and rolls down the window. There's a man wearing a light blue jumpsuit in the booth. He holds up his palm to them.

"Hello," he says warmly.

"Hi," Edwina says with a smile, "we're here for—"

"Are you pure of heart?" the man interrupts.

Edwina blinks, surprised. "Are we what? Uh, yes. We like to think so."

The man nods, approvingly, his palm still facing them. "Are you ready to confront wild truths?"

Edwina looks to Edwin, who is grinning.

"Oh yes. Yes, I am," he says.

"Great! You can pass through," the man responds.

He lowers his palm, and the gates begin to open.

"That's it? Those are the only security questions you have for us?" Edwin says.

For a top secret, never-been-seen-before institute, this security system seems pretty lax.

"Oh, no. Don't worry. I scanned your faces with my palm during those questions and we've received all your data that way. You're all cleared! Oh, no need to look alarmed, your data is incredibly protected. It will self-destruct from our database after you enter the gates. Onasander doesn't believe in data mining. Now, it'll just be another few minutes' drive through the forest until you reach the Institute's main buildings and the entrance. You'll know it when you see it, just follow the road."

He smiles and waves them on.

Edwina shakes her head, chuckles, and begins to drive through the gates. "I guess we better get used to some strangeness, huh?" she says. "I have a feeling that was as normal as this is going to get."

"I hope so," Edwin agrees.

They continue driving down a smoothly paved road between two forests. Except they're really more orchards than forests, Edwin notes. The trees are laid out in rows upon rows, somehow remaining neat and straight despite the winding road swerving back and forth between them.

There are fruits hanging from the trees. But what kind? Edwin doesn't recognize them. Some are shaped like cylinders, bright green. Other trees have turquoise fruit in the shape of little hearts. Maybe they're local to Montana?

"It's weird there aren't any other cars on the road," Edwin says. "We haven't passed anyone else."

"I'm sure we just can't see them because of the twists and turns," Edwina responds.

"Do you think we're late?"

"Nah, sweetie, we're right on time. Don't stress."

They drive in silence for a few moments, and then Edwina speaks. "So, how do you feel about being famous?"

Edwin startles.

"What do you mean, famous?"

"Well, everyone's talking about the OVAEO, and when it comes out that you're one of the handful of kids who passed it . . ."

It's true, of course, but Edwin hadn't even considered this. Famous? Would people really care about who passed the test? He realizes that if he hadn't passed the test, he would definitely want to know who did. The thought of fame makes him uncomfortable. He wonders who else is in this predicament with him.

"Don't you think that's why Onasander didn't release your names?" Edwina asks.

She's right, of course. Onasander knew the media would be all over those who passed the assessment, and he didn't want to expose them to any kind of media scrutiny before he'd had a chance to speak with them. He'd said as much in his letter.

How many kids passed the test? Edwin wonders for about the millionth time. Statistically, according to his calculations, given the difficulty of the assessment and his estimate of the percentage of kids around the country who had taken it, he hypothesized between twenty to fifty other students would be at the summit. A tiny amount, really.

"Do you think there will be other kids like me there, Mom?" Edwin asks softly.

Edwina looks at him, and he can see pinpricks of tears forming in her eyes. "Yes, honey. I think that there will be lots of brilliant kids who will just love to meet you. And who are special like you are."

Edwin nods silently and rolls down the window to breathe in the fresh air. The road winds through the forest, going up, up, up. The vastness of nature makes the mystery of this place feel even more intense. There's a swell of magic in the air. Edwin's never been somewhere so beautiful. It's so relaxing it makes him sleepy.

"Edwin, look," Edwina says softly.

Edwin didn't realize he'd closed his eyes. Now, shaken awake gently by his mother, he opens them and stretches, realizing the car has stopped. They're parked in a large circular driveway, with dozens of cars parked all around. In the center of the driveway is a statue of a hand, palm up. Above it floats an infinity symbol, as if the hand were holding it there by magic. The projection of the symbol transforms into Earth, then a sunflower, then a whale, then a test tube, then back to an infinity symbol. The symbol itself is larger than Edwin, the hand three times his size. The symbol keeps flickering and changing, and Edwin could stare at it all day, except there is even more to see. Edwin's eyes have become saucer-large. Edwina gets out of the car, and Edwin follows, his jaw dropping.

Here lies the Octagon Valley Institute.

The buildings are all set against the mountains, rising tall and majestic in the distance. It's a vast complex, part castle, part fortress, part government bunker, painted in colors so deep that they almost, but not quite, blend into the natural horizon. Burgundy turrets like those of medieval castles, the ones he spotted on the way in. Russian-style bulbous tower tops gleaming in indigo. Is that an emerald-green observatory with a huge telescope pointed out the window? The buildings all appear to be connected, each with different fantastical-looking spires, corridors, and bridges between them. Edwin figured the Institute would be huge, but he didn't anticipate anything like this. It doesn't look contemporary, not at all. It's as if each of the ancient civilizations of the world donated one of their most beautiful buildings to Onasander Octagon.

"Now this is what I call architecture!" Edwina looks around, approving.

She throws her arm around Edwin, and they laugh in amazement. They start walking away from the car, and it's only then that Edwin tears his eyes from the buildings and finally sees the people in front of him.

Kids.

Like him?

This is where it all begins.

Chapter Five

MEET THE PRESS?

Julie and her parents were the first to arrive at the Institute. They have been there since dawn, having taken an early flight from New York. Her parents, both professors, are always prompt and steady. They've packed bagged lunches and snacks, and right now the three of them are eating crackers, posture perfect, eyes observant, while the rest of the kids are standing around, gaping at the strange buildings of the Institute and sneaking glances at each other. So far, there are six of them. Julie's been counting.

They watch as a dented Honda makes its way to the drop-off. Turns out the guard at the gate told everyone what order they arrived in, and how many kids were ahead and behind them. He didn't tell that to Edwin. Perhaps he didn't want to make him feel bad for tardiness—after all, Onasander is famously tardy. *Important people don't rush; important people make other people rush* is his motto. Of course, that's what tardy people say to justify themselves.

Li'l Kimmy, wearing a long-sleeved T-shirt with a rhinestone exclamation mark on it, yells "Finally!" as Edwin steps out of the car. The guard told Li'l Kimmy she was the fourth out of eight, and she's been counting down ever since.

It seems rude, but in truth she's just expressing what everyone else has been feeling, and to be honest, Julie's a little thankful for that. Li'l Kimmy's talked so much while everyone's been waiting that Julie has barely had to utter a word.

The anticipation is intense as Edwin and his mother walk toward the group. "Come on, come on!" Li'l Kimmy says, waving at them.

Edwin smiles. "Hey."

"Hi there," Li'l Kimmy says in her exuberant manner. "I'm Eun-Kyung Kim, but you can call me Li'l Kimmy. What's your name? We've already all introduced ourselves."

"I'm Edwin," says Edwin.

"What up, Edwin," says Li'l Kimmy. She points to Julie, standing anxiously between her two parents. Finished with her snack, she's now tapping her fingers like she's playing the piano on her thighs. Julie knows it might appear odd to others, but she can't help it. It calms her. At least a little.

"That's Julie," Li'l Kimmy says.

"Hi, Edwin," says Julie, so quietly he can barely hear her.

"Hey," says Edwin, feeling relieved someone else looks as nervous as he feels.

Then Li'l Kimmy points to a boy with a video game console in front of his face. "That's Anton."

Anton ignores them and keeps playing. His device makes *beep* and *blurp* sounds, and once in a while Anton curses under his breath.

An Indian boy with dark wavy hair ambles over and puts his hand out. "Hey, I'm Dilip Aggarwal," he says, shaking Edwin's hand. "And for the record, I don't understand how I passed the assessment. Just want to get that clear right away."

Edwin laughs.

A dark-haired Filipino girl tugs on her mom's sweater and asks her a question quietly. The two confer as if discussing nuclear codes.

"That's Ting-Ting," Li'l Kimmy says, "and that's Harold." She points to a yellow-haired boy wearing a suit and a scowl, standing between two human tanks in dark sunglasses who can only be his bodyguards.

Since Ting-Ting is in a deep conversation with her mother and Harold ignores them, Edwin just nods.

"I think that's all of us," says Li'l Kimmy with a casual shrug. "Or wait . . ." She starts counting on her fingers.

Just then, another car pulls up: a black Tesla Model X, and the right falcon wing unfurls to reveal a white girl with glossy brown hair under a plaid headband. She's wearing a blue blazer and a matching plaid skirt, like a school uniform. Gossip Girl come to life.

Eight, thinks Julie. *There's eight of us. Eight sides to an octagon. Coincidence?* (Yes, it is. She doesn't know the truth about Harold.)

"Hello hello," the new girl says, strutting up to them. "Maureen Pearson. What did I miss? Any of the reporters here yet? Don't tell me I missed talking to the reporters!"

She's followed by two men, whom Edwin presumes are her dads. They saunter confidently slightly behind her, whispering to each other and sizing up the other kids and their guardians. At first, Edwin thinks they're judging everyone, but then they smile and start introducing themselves. Friendly in the way people from certain parts of New York and LA are friendly—like they're trying to figure out if you're useful.

Maureen, meanwhile, pouts a little, and Julie wonders what she's talking about. Reporters? Oh right, she forgot, this is a media moment! But no worries. As a child prodigy, she's had a lot of experience talking to the press, and she's found magazine and television interviews far more relaxing than talking to kids her own age. At least with the media, the dynamic is clear.

Julie's had many media accolades—making *Time*'s "5 Under 5" list, *New York Magazine*'s "Elementary Kids to Watch," and even the cover of *Vanity Fair*'s Playground issue. And every single one of the reporters told her she gave an excellent interview.

Now that all the kids have arrived, the very reporters Maureen wished for suddenly come out of the woodwork. Or rather, their cars. So that's why there were so many cars for so few people! They approach the group in a wave of gray suits and notepads. Cameras start flashing, and serious-looking journalists wielding microphones and voice recorders begin asking a multitude of questions in an overwhelming flurry. There are newscasters with full camera crews, boom mikes, and lighting technicians.

"How does it feel to be one of only eight students in the country to pass the OVAEO?"

"What's your name, and where did you come from?"

"How high is your IQ?"

"How long did you study for the assessment?"

"Was it possible to cheat?"

"Did you always know you were superhumanly smart?"

"What do you think of the other participants?"

"How do you plan to save the world?"

The kids try to answer, but it's too hard to be heard above the noise.

"Um . . ." says Dilip.

"I don't cheat . . ." begins Edwin.

"I'm not really that smart," hedges Ting-Ting, looking at her mother nervously.

"You'll have to ask my publicist," sneers Harold.

"Excuse me," snaps Maureen. "You're stepping on my foot!"

A loud, piercing whistle emanates through the two fingers pressed between Li'l Kimmy's lips. "Yo, yo, yo!" she calls. She turns to Julie. "Okay, go."

Julie clears her throat. She'd asked Li'l Kimmy to help get the reporters' attention. She knows what to do with a press conference.

"Can we get a little more organized here, please?" Julie says. "We can't answer all your questions at once. You." She points to a woman with her pen poised. "Why don't you start with one question?"

"What was in the letter you got from Onasander Octagon?" the reporter asks.

"We were asked not to disclose that," Julie answers.

"Come on!" the woman prods. "Give us a hint."

"Hey." Li'l Kimmy steps up next to Julie. "Back off."

She's getting dangerously close to emoting. Anger is something she does not display. *Keep it cool, Li'l Kimmy.*

"Look, kid. We all drove a long way to get this story," the reporter says with a sneer. "'No comment' isn't going to cut it."

And then Li'l Kimmy has an idea.

"Oh, really?" She takes out her iPhone and snaps a pic of the reporter. "This will be so funny for my Insta," she says, posting the picture to her story with the text *Ambushed by the press!* She holds the picture up to the reporter. "How does it feel to be on the other side? My five thousand adoring fans are going to rip you to shreds."

Julie can't help but laugh.

It's funny how absurd this is.

Not the reporter—she's dealt with intrusive reporters before.

The *really* absurd thing? Julie just met someone her own age whom she actually likes.

Chapter Six

THE ONE AND ONLY OUTRAGEOUS ONASANDER OCTAGON

After Li'l Kimmy posts her picture, the reporters only get louder, meaner, and more insistent. They are not used to being talked back to by kids, but then, they'd never met Li'l Kimmy, had they? But the raucous chatter, flashing of cameras, and rat-a-tat-tat questioning comes to a halt when the double-height, ornately carved wooden doors of the Institute suddenly open—smoothly, noiselessly, not at all creaky and crackly like one would have expected. At the doorway stands a tall, thin man in a light blue three-piece suit, wearing silver aviators on the bridge of his long nose. His white hair poofs out in all directions. His skin is dark brown, and when he takes off his sunglasses, his eyes are so bright they look violet. In a surprise to all, he looks startlingly young, the white hair an affectation—it could easily have been pink or blue. He walks with a bounce in his step, almost as if he's walking on air. He is multiracial, and under various lighting and angles could pass for any number of ethnicities—Nigerian or Irish, or Spanish, or Persian, or Chinese. He could be fifteen, twenty-five, or a very young fifty. *Timeless*, that's the word. Is *raceless* one too?

Edwin shivers, and Edwina squeezes his hand. They're both starstruck. Here he is, Onasander Octagon, in the flesh. Some people say that famous people look shorter in person, but Edwin's pretty sure that Onasander looks taller.

"That will be quite enough," Onasander Octagon chastises the reporters. "I agreed to let you on the premises for five minutes, and your five minutes are up. Kindly exit Octagon Valley."

"But we barely got an answer yet!" an annoyed journalist complains.

"How are we supposed to write an article from that?" another chimes in.

"We need five more minutes!" yet another seethes.

"Your time-management failures are not my concern," Onasander replies serenely, crossing his arms and smiling slightly. "We had an agreement. Off you go. Toodle-oo!"

Julie appreciates how calmly Onasander handles the situation. It's clear he's wary of all the media interest. She's had to sit through so many interviews on behalf of the orchestra that she honestly forgot that not engaging with the press is always an option.

The reporters appear stunned at this turn of events but, in the presence of Onasander's steely resolve, do as they are told, quietly clicking off their recording devices and putting the lens caps on their cameras. They shuffle off to their vehicles and drive away, leaving the eight kids and their companions alone with the mysterious inventor.

"Now that that unpleasantness is over with." Onasander smiles. "Welcome, everyone, to the Octagon Valley Institute! It is a true honor to have you here. Please say your goodbyes to your guardians. This is where they leave you."

The eight kids turn to their people. Harold dismisses his bodyguards. Maureen's two dads kiss her cheeks, and she snaps in a whiny voice, "Don't mess up my blowout!"

Her dads cower. "Sorry, sorry," they murmur. "Sorry, precious." It's clear who runs that family. The French have a word for it: *l'enfant roi* or *l'enfant terrible*. (Guttural *r*'s, *s'il vous plaît*!)

Ting-Ting's mother has to be physically detached from Ting-Ting by Ting-Ting's father. "Let her go now, come on." Can hands look like claws? Asking for a friend.

Julie gives her parents a tight hug. Her parents are her best friends, as sweet and pathetic as that is. She tries to remind herself that it will only be three short days with these other kids, and if they all hate her like her classmates do, it's only a few days to suffer through until she can be back with her family.

Dilip gives his parents and siblings high fives. "See you guys soon!"

Li'l Kimmy and her cousin Sully fist-bump before Sully pulls her in for a hug. "You know you're missing a great festival this weekend," she teases.

"Here's hoping this thing is worth it, then," Li'l Kimmy whispers in her ear, and they giggle.

Anton does not look up from his video game to say goodbye to his parents. "Shhhh! I'm two hundred points away from leveling up!" he groans. He's a charmer, that one!

Edwin turns around to look at Edwina and catches a glimpse of her brushing a tear from her eye. "You got this, Edwin. I'll be here to pick you up in three days. I'm so, so proud of you."

Edwin says goodbye to his mom, suddenly feeling like it's the first day of kindergarten and he can't let go. This all feels so huge. He's supposed to just walk into this Institute alone? Well, not alone, exactly, but with seven other kids he's only just met? He's struck with utter terror, but his mother pulls away, kisses the top of his head, and squeezes his shoulders.

Onasander claps, rousing everyone from their goodbyes. "Come on, now," he says. "It's all beginning. It's all beginning."

He turns and walks through the doorway, into the foyer of the building, waving for the eight of them to follow.

It's only three days, Edwin thinks to himself with a sigh. He waves to Edwina, who walks toward their car, and he takes a step forward. Three days. What could happen in three days?

What, indeed!

He's about to find out.

Chapter Seven

CHILL AND *SO* NOT CHILL

As soon as the front doors close and they're alone in the foyer, Onasander turns around. Edwin's a bit taken aback. Onasander has a huge grin on his face.

"Oh, I'm just so excited!" he squeals. "Are we all excited?"

He clasps his hands together and giggles, flashing dimples on each of his cheeks.

The eight kids stare at their strange benefactor. Onasander's demeanor has completely transformed. The man barely cracks a smile on TV. During his Octo Talks or on newscasts, he's always placid, relaxed, neutral, even-keeled. Need another descriptor? Essentially, it's agreed upon: He's impossible to crack. Li'l Kimmy always tells people he seems like an uptight snob. So this manic giggling seems a touch off-brand. This certainly is not the Onasander she's seen on TV. Maybe this place will be more interesting than she thought.

"I'm getting ahead of myself." Onasander shakes his head and grins. "Let's keep going."

Onasander leads the eight stunned and silent kids through the foyer of the Institute.

"This place is baller," Li'l Kimmy whispers to Dilip as they follow him inside.

The room has huge ceilings, higher than the biggest arena or stadium she's ever seen. There are skylights, so the whole room is lit up with sunlight. In the center, a large fountain with ornately carved figures spouts sparkling water in an endless rush. Around the perimeter of the foyer are a dozen doors. The floors are white marble, and there are benches positioned all around facing random pieces of artwork, some impressionist, some modern, some abstract, some computer generated, and one that seems to be moving. . . .

"Yeah, I guess," Dilip says, looking at her and shrugging, frowning slightly.

What's his problem? Li'l Kimmy thinks. She thought Dilip seemed cool, but he's distracted, unimpressed. No more descriptors needed there.

Li'l Kimmy knew who Onasander was before he announced the assessment, of course. Everyone did. But she wasn't obsessed with him the way she knows some kids are. She's more than just a brain! Her parents insisted she take the assessment. Of course she had to, she's Korean! Her parents went to cram schools in Seoul. There was no getting around it. And when she passed it? Well, there was no negotiating. She had to come here, even if she's missing a music festival she really wants to attend. But hey, it's only three days, right? Music festivals in LA are like waves on Venice Beach: You wait a few beats, and another one comes along.

So she decided to use these three days to her advantage. If Onasander Octagon really has an in with the hip-hop world, she's going to get close to this odd man and make some connections. That's one thing she's learned from living in LA: It's all about networking!

Maybe Dilip didn't want to come here either. And maybe he's yet to figure out how to spin it to his advantage.

Dilip's approach to the OVAEO was quite different from the others. He doesn't have the supernatural smarts of Edwin, nor does he feel the need to get away from horrible classmates like Julie. But Dilip had heard about Onasander's hoverboard prototypes that were in development and knew that he needed to see them up close. Any surfer would've given their left arm (if they hadn't already lost it to a shark) to check out the hoverboard prototypes. Plus, he knew his parents would be really proud if he passed. So he had to at least give it a try.

His approach was like that of a gambler, though Dilip

THE (SUPER SECRET) OCTAGON VALLEY SOCIETY

would probably frame it, if asked by his parents or teachers, as experimenting with the principles of probability. Basically, he decided to circle all the answers at random and hope for the best.

Li'l Kimmy was sort of right in this regard: He's gotten quite good at learning how to put the right spin on his approach to life. This is because Dilip has his own way of doing things, even if that way doesn't usually match up with the expectations of those around him.

His classroom in Newport Beach, California, has a clear view of the ocean. For many people this would be a selling point. But for Dilip's parents, it's an unfortunate fact of life. Not because they don't love the ocean, but because they didn't immigrate to America just for their son to stare longingly at waves lapping the shore all day, envisioning what fun he would be having if he were surfing instead of spacing out so hard that he forgets what subject he's even supposed to be paying attention to. They moved to America for opportunity! And their son only wants to have fun! It's so disappointing. The ocean and the beach hold far more intrigue for Dilip than a classroom ever has. He's what some people might call a kinesthetic learner, but even a kinesthetic learner is expected to finish their math homework.

On the day of the OVAEO (NOT an olive oil), the waves were looking particularly divine. With his pencil poised over the paper and his eyes looking out the window, he couldn't help but envision what new tricks he would be able to pull on those bodacious crests. He looked back to the assessment. Who was he kidding? He's a solid C student. He was never going to ace this assessment anyway! He didn't have a snowball's chance in a microwave. Though his heart dipped slightly as he thought about how happy his parents would be if he aced it, he sighed, knowing that would never happen. It just wasn't in the cards. He hedged his bets, figured out his odds, and circled the answers at random. He circled all the way to the bottom of the last page, quickly, without thinking too hard, then stood up.

Lunchtime is the best time to surf, after all. He'd have the whole beach to himself.

But somehow, by some strange miracle of fate, he aced the test. He still doesn't understand how. If he's being honest, he thinks that there might have been a glitch in the system, or some kind of mistake, though Onasander doesn't seem like the kind of guy who makes mistakes. This feeling was only amplified when Dilip met the other kids. They're, well, dorky. No, that's not nice, he knows. It's just his defense mechanisms kicking in.

But it's obvious the rest of them are brainiacs. He's not.

He feels unworthy of being here. He's been eavesdropping, and this Edwin kid seems like the type of genius who'd be a chess master in the womb. And what's up with that sixth-grader who's a conductor? These kids are intense. Even that rapper girl who talks a mile a minute. The only thing Dilip is intense about is surfing. With every step, he's questioning what he's doing here. He doesn't belong with these straight-A students. He's a C student with lucky odds. How can he admit this to Onasander? It feels like he's about to be found out at any moment.

This is why he's kind of rude to Li'l Kimmy. Feeling unworthy has a tendency to make people act that way, too.

Maureen, on the other hand, *knows* she is worthy. Perhaps she's a little too sure of that fact. As they walk, she's peppering Onasander with question after question. "Is this the only entrance to Octagon Valley?" she asks briskly, as if she's assessing its real-estate value. "What do you call this room, Mr. Octagon? Where do all these doors go?"

"All in due time, Maureen, and please, call me Onasander," Onasander says, with what can only be described as extreme patience.

"I'm sorry, Onasander, it's just that I'm so excited. I'm a huge admirer," she says sweetly. "Where do you source the materials to build everything, by the way? And what's the deal with these fountains? Does anyone else work here? Where are they now?"

Onasander just chuckles, but that doesn't stop Maureen from continuing to press.

Maureen Pearson is an Upper East Side local. Please don't get it confused: Not *all* of New York is worth her time. She wouldn't be caught dead on the subway that Julie routinely takes to work, although she and her dads frequent the Philharmonic. And the opera. And pretty much every Broadway show. Yes, it's true, Maureen is the queen of New York, flitting from social function to social function. And no, she's not talking about school dances or anything so basic as that. Though if she had to go to a school dance, her all-girls prep school would be the place for it. At least then it would be *classy*.

Maureen Pearson is head girl at her school, which comes as no surprise. She didn't even have any competition. She has her whole life planned out. What's the plan, you ask? Oh, you thought she'd tell you? No, no. She doesn't share that kind of precious information with the masses. You'll just have to keep on reading for that, sweetie. But rest assured, Maureen has it all planned out. How to have her perfect life, just like her perfect dads. The kind of people who never have a hair out of place, never a wrinkle to be found—on a shirt or, heaven forbid, a face.

The day of the OVAEO, Maureen wasn't concerned when she click-clacked in her Louboutin kitten heels into the wood-paneled classroom of her prep school. This assessment was going to be a breeze. Who could be smarter than Maureen? She's the most prepared, the most precocious, the most dedicated, and, don't forget, the most naturally gifted sixth-grader in the country! She's sure of it. Oh, and she's ready to be ruthless, too. Just like her dads, who built a plastic-surgery empire that plumped the lips and hoovered off the hips of everyone this side of Park Avenue. She'll cover up any mean words with a glossy pink smile. She's a girlboss!

Maureen already knows about the 108th question, and the truth about the Octagon Institute. Don't understand what she's talking about? Keep up, honey! Or else!

One day, everyone will hail the queen.

That would be Maureen.

Know what I mean?

Chapter Eight

CHEATERS NEVER WIN?

Maureen's inner monologue thankfully comes to a stop when Onasander arrives at the center fountain and suddenly turns around to face them, his eyes full of childish glee.

"It's happening! It's finally happening!" Onasander claps again, smiling wider. "This is a very exciting day! The day when you eight—or, well, seven . . . Harold, I'm not sure exactly how you ended up here. . . . Hold on, how *did* you end up here?"

The seven of them look at Harold, whose nose is literally stuck up in the air. Li'l Kimmy thinks he looks like he just smelled something rotten, but this seems to be his permanent expression.

"My father—" he starts.

"Ah, yes, your father. Your father has been a great donor over the years. But I am not sure why this warrants you entrance to the Institute? You did cheat on the assessment, after all, did you not, Harold?"

The color drains from Harold's face as he sputters a nonanswer.

Busted! Li'l Kimmy holds in a laugh. This is already more exciting than she was expecting.

"Hold on," Edwin interjects. "If you cheated, how did you make it through the gate?" *Didn't we have to swear we were pure of heart?*

"Gate?" Harold mutters, still reeling from being found out. "I was helicoptered in."

"Yes, Harold, I know about the cheating," Onasander sighs. "There must have been quite a security breach for you to acquire assessment answers."

He claps a third time and several staff members in the same powder-blue jumpsuits as the security guard appear, walking single file out of one of the automated doors. His research scientists and assistants, one presumes.

"Find the leak," he tells them, and they retreat. "But you know what, Harold, I'm in such a great mood today, with these brilliant young minds here, I'll give you a shot. Why not! We'll see how you fare."

"I am outraged by this accusation!" Harold snips. "I'll be calling my father—"

"No, no, I'm sure you won't, Harold!" Onasander shakes his head. "Not today, and not until you leave."

Harold stares at Onasander, his face slowly turning purple.

No one talks to Harold like that.

Harold *always* gets his way.

Because Harold, as if you didn't already know, is Harold Postman Jr. VIII of *the* Harold Postman line. Oh, you haven't heard of them? Are you sure? That's simply astonishing! Frankly, Harold wouldn't believe it if you told him that. After all, his great-great-great-great-great-great-great grandfather founded what has become a multi-bazillion-dollar company. It has holdings and interests far and wide, for goodness' sake! You sure you haven't heard of him? Well, surely you *have* heard of the Octagon Institute. The Postmans happen to be the primary benefactors of the Institute. They practically own the place! So Harold *deserves* to pass the OVAEO, right? He deserves to go to the Octagon Valley three-day summit, right? He deserves anything he wants, right? Right?! *RIGHT?!*

The day of the assessment, sitting in his cashmere sweater at his oak-wood desk in the most expensive private school in the country, Harold pulled out the pre-completed OVAEO from his leather shoulder bag and brought it to the front of the class.

Rules don't apply to him. He's a Postman, after all!

Not that Onasander cares about this one bit. Postman? Isn't that the guy who delivers the mail? And believe me, the postman is a lot more useful than Harold Postman Jr. VIII. Onasander clears his throat and turns sternly to all of the kids.

"I have a no-phones policy here at the Octagon Valley Institute. You'll quickly notice that these devices are not at all operative here. A pity—or shall we say, a miracle!"

The kids all take their phones out of their pockets and bags to see if he's telling the truth.

"He's right!" Dilip says, holding his phone in his hand. On the black screen, there's a palm holding up the silver infinity symbol, pulsing. No one's ever seen an Apple or Android make that symbol before.

"If your phones are truly more important to you than this weekend, of course I can arrange for your guardians to come back and pick you up," Onasander offers. "Though you will of course spend the rest of your lives wondering what might have happened if you hadn't prioritized those insipid little devices. . . . Not to be dramatic!"

Onasander laughs, pulling himself out of what was surely about to be a diatribe against mass addiction to phones. That one's for another time.

Ting-Ting looks as if she's seriously considering the matter.

Li'l Kimmy shrugs. Three days without a phone? Sure,

she'll miss her SoundCloud and her Spotify, but she can always make her own music.

Maureen is scowling at her phone but puts it away like everyone else.

"I don't really care much for cell phones anyway," Julie says softly. She didn't even take hers out of her bag to check.

Edwin doesn't even own a phone. He only has an iPad, which is at home.

"NO!" Anton shouts.

The others all look at him in surprise. He flushes. "Well, what about, like, other devices?" he asks sheepishly. "Like gaming devices?"

It had taken him a moment to process what Onasander had said because he was so close to securing a new life in his game, and he didn't process things properly in such high-adrenaline situations.

"I doubt you'll have any time for that, Anton!" Onasander chuckles.

Anton checks his gaming console and, seeing it's still working, breathes a sigh of relief. "Oh, we're good. I'm good. All good."

He might've had to leave if he didn't have access to his games all weekend.

Bit of background about Anton? He's a simple kid with simple wants. And what he simply wants is to be left alone so he can lose himself in the myriad of real-time strategy, RPG, and FPS games that he keeps on rotation. He may as well be wearing a T-shirt at all times that reads I'D RATHER BE GAMING. But honestly, you don't need a T-shirt to tell you that. His sour expression, crossed arms, and general disengagement when his gaming console is far away are enough to give anyone a clue. His most natural habitat is his bedroom, where he has a deluxe setup his parents bought him after weeks of begging. On the rare occasion that he's not in his bedroom, he'll settle for a portable gaming device. But it is rare, the occasion that he's not in his bedroom. He is homeschooled, after all, so he barely has to leave the blissful boundaries of his room/cave.

One day, Anton's fingers will merge with his game console, and it will be the happiest day of his life. Man and machine are a match made in heaven, if you ask him.

All that time he's spent gaming isn't totally for naught, though. He's picked up an incredible capacity to multitask, so he can do his homeschool work and game at the same time. He's also picked up a lot of trivia, thanks to the diversity of the games he plays. He aces his homeschool assignments easily. The multitasking really came in handy as he filled out the online version of the OVAEO on one screen and played his most recent video game on the other screen.

Oh yeah, of course he has two screens, how else would he be a Twitch streamer?

Chapter Nine

THE WELCOME, ETC.

Now that all the children have discovered their phones are inoperable, Onasander resumes the tour. "Wonderful. Now that that's settled, well, here we are!" He twirls around, his arms stretched out wide and his face to the ceiling.

"Isn't it magnificent?" he asks when he stops spinning. "As you can see, this is our grand foyer, the entrance of the whole Institute. As I'm sure you could tell on your way in, we have rather a lot of buildings."

"Yeah, what are they all for? Will we get a tour of all of them?" Maureen asks.

"Again, all in due time, Maureen, all in due time." Onasander begins walking across the foyer, past the fountain, and to one of the large doors that line the perimeter of the room, and the eight kids follow him.

"So what kind of rap music do you like?" Dilip hears Julie ask Li'l Kimmy.

"Well, I definitely like girl rappers, to start . . ." Li'l Kimmy answers, and then Dilip can't hear any more, as they walk several paces ahead of him.

Dilip looks around at the other kids. Sort of a motley crew. He wonders whether he has anything at all in common with them. There's no way Edwin or Anton could skate in the shoes they're wearing, so he supposes that's out. Li'l Kimmy seems cool, but does she ever stop talking? Maureen looks like she's never spent a day outside New York in her life. The closest thing she's seen to nature is probably the Natural History Museum.

"Hey," Edwin says shyly to him. Dilip thinks he looks pretty nervous. He tries to set him at ease.

"Hey, dude. So, you excited about this whole thing?"

"Oh. Yes, I'm extremely excited. I've been a fan of Onasander's for years," Edwin gushes. "What about you?"

"I heard he has some sick hoverboard tech somewhere in here, and I'm just hoping I get to see it," Dilip says. "Honestly, I can't believe I made it here. I'm not, like, a straight-A student or anything."

"Wow. I am, and I studied for, like, three weeks straight," says Edwin.

Dilip's throat feels dry. What the heck is he doing here? There's no way he did as well on the assessment as this kid.

"Whoa. You're hardcore!" Dilip forces a smile and gives Edwin a friendly slap on the shoulder. "I barely studied. But I just got this sort of feeling while I was taking the test. It probably sounds weird. I don't know, I just felt, like, in a flow, or something."

This is the truth, but Dilip still doesn't get it. He was basically guessing on half the questions. He doesn't even know why he's telling Edwin this.

"Huh," Edwin says, looking at Dilip intently. "I think I know exactly what you mean."

"After you!" Onasander says, holding a door open for them.

The eight kids file into a darkened room with red leather couches and walls lined with bookshelves. It's dim, apparently lit exclusively by candlelight—a chandelier of candles overhead and candelabras on every surface. It's so completely the opposite of the bright white room they were just in, it takes a moment for everyone's eyes to adjust. Edwin's immediate worry is the room's apparent lack of fire safety. But the effect is so magical, he lets those worries go. Once they're all seated, Onasander closes the door behind him and walks to the front of the room.

"So," he begins, smiling, clapping his hands excitedly. "You are all probably wondering what this weekend will look like. You've seen the schedules, of course, but I'm sure you have a lot of questions."

The kids nod, and Ting-Ting's hand shoots into the air.

"Oh! You really do have questions! Okay, I suppose we can do just one question now. Yes, Ting-Ting?"

"What does 'The Welcome, Etc.' from the schedule mean? Are we in that right now? Is this The Welcome, Etc.?" she asks.

"Why, yes it is," Onasander replies. "Yes it is."

Ting-Ting beams.

Anabelle "Ting-Ting" Costanza prides herself on asking all the right questions and knowing how to butter up the host. From a young age, her mother drilled into her that life isn't just about knowing facts, it's about kissing up. That's right, sucking up to authority at all costs. A little brown-nosing never hurt anyone, and hey, if you get special treatment as a result, who can blame you?

It's not that Ting-Ting doesn't necessarily deserve all her marks. She's smart, absolutely. But she's also ensured that she's every teacher's favorite pet. Her placid smile and perfect ponytail work wonders for proving to her teachers that she's just the kind of girl who should get an A.

So when Ting-Ting didn't pass the OVAEO, her mother just wasn't having it. Her daughter, Ting-Ting, apple of the teacher's eye, didn't pass? How could this be possible? Ting-Ting brought the graded assessment home, shoved shamefully in the bottom of her backpack, hoping to hide it. But her mother rifled through the backpack and found the assessment, scanning for what Ting-Ting missed.

And, lo and behold, there it was.

Remember, there's something very particular about the OVAEO. Of course, the 107 questions of the assessment are very difficult and challenging for the best and brightest of minds. But even answering everything correctly is not enough to pass the OVAEO. No. There's something else, remember? Quiz time: In the first chapter of the book, we told you what it was. Think about it. Don't you dare look at the next couple of lines. Think. Got it? Good job, dear reader. In order to be successful at the OVAEO, you have to answer the *108th* question. Doesn't seem too hard, does it? Well, here's the thing. Not everyone can *see* the 108th question. Not just answer it, but see it.

If you can see this question, if you notice it and attempt to answer it, then that is what indicates that not only are you a genius in your own right, but you're Extra. Extra in every sense of the word. Extra-ordinary. Extra-vagant in your abilities. Extra-special. And something else extra, too. . . . But hold it right there.

Let's get back to Ting-Ting.

Ting-Ting didn't see the 108th question. (And neither did Harold, the little cheater.)

Of course, Ting-Ting's mom did some digging after reviewing her daughter's assessment. She couldn't understand why she hadn't passed it. After vigorous research (i.e., harassing the beleaguered homeroom teacher), Ting-Ting's mom finally uncovered the truth of the 108th question.

She was relentless in her petition to the school to give Ting-Ting a redo until they finally caved, and voilà: That time, Ting-Ting passed.

Her mother's persistence is—what's that word?

Extra-Ordinary.

"So what's the 'et cetera' part of the welcome?" Maureen wants to know.

Onasander taps his chin. His childlike glee has waned a bit now that he's tasked with explanations.

"An interesting and pertinent question. Well, let me start with this. We have a lot planned for you this weekend. It is my hope that by the end of the weekend, you will feel as though your lives have changed, and for the better. We want to give you a taste of all the branches of the Octagon Valley Institute—and there are a lot!"

Sitting on the red leather couch, Dilip taps his foot in a quick rhythm and catches Edwin's eye. Edwin's foot is shaking too. He grins. Seems Dilip's not the only one with a nervous tic.

"But I have something to ask of you before we get to all the workshops, lectures, and seminars we have planned for this weekend. One last assessment."

Six of them look at each other, astonished. Harold stares

straight ahead. Anton jams the buttons on his video game.

Ting-Ting's hand shoots up again.

"Just a minute, Ting-Ting. Let me explain a little," Onasander says, beginning to pace at the front of the room. "So yes, I have one last assessment for you. One that will undoubtedly surprise and delight! This will be quite unlike the one that you took in your classrooms. It's more of a real-life obstacle course! Obstacle courses are fun, aren't they? Just ask the ancient Greeks! It will involve teamwork, as well as using your individual strengths. I promise, once you complete the course, it will all make sense, and you will understand why I've asked this of you. You may even be shocked by the results. But this experience will also introduce you to another side of the Octagon Valley Institute, one that no one even knows exists!"

Edwin feels a rush of surprise and delight, just like Onasander's letter had promised.

"This is a scavenger hunt, if you will, through the most top secret of all the top secret parts of the Octagon Valley Institute compound. You will need to find eight puzzle pieces, which you will acquire by passing certain challenges. To pass these challenges, you'll all need to use your unique and individual talents. Once you've found all eight puzzle pieces, you can put them together, and they will lead you to where the ultimate prize lies. I will be waiting for you there."

"Sounds fun!" Li'l Kimmy smiles.

"That's the spirit, Li'l Kimmy!" Onasander grins. "Now, any questions?"

Every kid besides Anton raises their hand.

"I'd like to call my father," Harold shouts.

Onasander laughs and ignores him. "You know what? I think this will go better without answers to these questions. All you need to know is what I've told you." He claps. "Now, if you wouldn't mind, I have a bit of an odd request. How would you all feel about being blindfolded?"

Chapter Ten

THE GAME IS AFOOT!

Dilip has never been blindfolded before. Come to think of it, though, it could be interesting to skateboard blindfolded. He's heard about honing your intuitive skills. He's pretty much mastered the kickflip, the backside 360, every kind of ollie, and most ramp tricks. Maybe going in blindfolded could open him up to a whole new world of skateboarding.

Julie does not like being blindfolded. Who does? First off, it's really dark. The eight of them are holding on to a thick velvet rope, soft under their hands. Julie believes Onasander is leading them as they walk, but she supposes there's no way to know for sure, since no one is speaking and she can't, well, see anything.

They turn right, left, right, left, left, left, right, right, for what seems like ten minutes. Well, it doesn't seem like ten minutes. It is ten minutes. As a conductor, Julie has an excellent sense of time. Not that that necessarily comes in handy, in this case, since knowing how long they walked for doesn't get her any closer to knowing where she is now and what they're supposed to do.

Finally, she hears the sound of a door opening. She feels a hand on her back, guiding her, presumably, through the door. When Onasander explained the scavenger hunt, she was excited. But now she has a creepy sensation washing over her. As it turns out, she doesn't like being without her sense of sight. You learn something new about yourself every day, apparently! And whose hand is this, anyway? Why does it feel like it's not attached to a body?

The hand stops her from taking any more steps. Then it pushes down on her shoulder, seeming to indicate she sit. It's strange, trusting this disembodied hand instructing her to sit, when she can't see that a chair will be there to catch her. But it is. She sits. Then, a minute later, there's the sound of a door closing.

Julie decides to take her blindfold off. She prefers to have all her senses, thank you very much. She blinks, waiting for her eyes to adjust to the fluorescent white lights. She and each of the seven other kids are seated at desks, each desk a different weird shape.

"Uh, are we supposed to take the blindfolds off now?"

Li'l Kimmy says, taking hers off and kicking her feet up onto the strangely shaped desk. "What next?"

It's a good question, Julie thinks. Onasander is nowhere in sight. He bid them farewell as soon as they got the blindfolds on. No sign of his light-blue-jumpsuit-wearing staff of scientists and researchers either.

A strange energy has fallen over the small, stuffy waiting room, the kids blinking and rubbing their eyes. What are they waiting for, exactly? Are they in competition with one another? Anton, who's put his video game console aside for a moment, certainly seems to think so. He's studying each of them as if they're his opponents in his game. And maybe they are?

It's clear Harold, Maureen, and Ting-Ting have come to the same conclusion. They all have their hackles up, ready to do whatever it takes to get ahead.

But didn't Onasander say that they're supposed to be working together to find the puzzle pieces? This doesn't seem like the kind of test where they have to beat each other. It kind of sounds like they have to work together, which means this is just another group project.

Julie hates group projects. Either no one in the group listens to her, or everyone exexpects her to do all the work. She's been bullied pretty much ever since she can remember, and in every way that you can imagine. (Her school is old-fashioned and hasn't yet discovered that bullying no longer exists.) She was sort of hoping that this weekend might feel like an escape. So far, she can't tell how likely that is.

Dilip seems unconcerned, while Li'l Kimmy is quiet for once.

"Anyone else feel like it was weird that we had to be blindfolded to get here?" Maureen asks. "What was that about? I wanted to see the corridors!"

"I'm sure Onasander had his reasons," Edwin replies.

"You're really obsessed with him, aren't you?" Maureen asks, raising an eyebrow judgmentally. "Why are you still blindfolded?"

Edwin feels exposed, suddenly. "Aren't we all obsessed with him?" he asks in a quiet voice.

"Not really," Maureen says. "I mean, obviously he's super famous. Being associated with him gives us clout." She tosses her hair over her shoulder.

"If that's what matters to you," Edwin replies.

Julie wants to speak up but feels too shy. She's on the same page as Edwin. Coming here, meeting Onasander, it's pretty much the most exciting thing that's ever happened to her. If only she could say so out loud. It pains her to look at Edwin so dejected. Maybe she can say something. Agree with him. Back him up. Maybe . . .

"So, when do you guys think someone's going to come get us?" Dilip asks.

Then: the clicking noise of the gold door locking. Then: the panic.

"It's locked!"

"What's going on?"

"Why is it so hot all of a sudden . . . ?"

"Are we trapped?!"

But why would Onasander trap us? Edwin wonders. It's not like anyone was trying to leave *before* the door locked. It must just be part of the test. He's not worried. Why should he worry? It's Onasander. He has everything under control. Doesn't he?

Until . . .

"Hello again, Octos. Welcome to the *real* Octagon Valley Institute," Onasander's voice says over the loudspeakers.

Cue the darkness, then the screams.

(And still no ice cream.)

(Alas!)

PART TWO:
ONASANDER'S
OBSTACLES

Chapter Eleven

THE GREAT DIVIDE

When the lights come up again, the screaming stops. Harold is crouched in the corner, a terrified look on his face. Li'l Kimmy has her hands protectively over her head. Dilip is scowling. Julie has the look of a hunted deer. Ting-Ting is under a desk. Even Maureen looks rattled. Anton—you know what Anton's doing by now. Edwin, well, Edwin's just trying to take it all in.

"Onasander?" he calls, but there's no response.

"What did he mean by the *real* Octagon Valley Institute?" Dilip says, standing up quickly.

Edwin needs a moment to regroup here. Only minutes ago, he was certain that this was the start of the best weekend of his life. Even if he was still battling his nerves, he felt like this weekend would change things for him. Well, it looks like it will certainly change things, but not in the way he had hoped.

That darkness they just experienced was weird—when the light came back on, it felt almost like they weren't even in the same room anymore.

"I don't get it," Li'l Kimmy says. "Is this a joke of some kind? Is Onasander playing a joke on us?"

"Look, let's just call our parents," Harold says, adjusting his tie. "They'll get us out of this."

"Don't you remember? Our phones don't work, genius," snaps Maureen.

"Yeah, no one's coming for us," says Li'l Kimmy. "Not until Monday."

"Whoa!" Anton yells.

They all turn to him excitedly.

"I just got a new high score!"

They turn away.

Julie sighs. Like the rest, she thought Anton was finally paying attention to what was happening.

"Wait, wait, wait," Ting-Ting says, standing up, voice wavering. "Are we going to, like, die?! I can't die! I haven't even finished middle school! I still need to get into Harvard! If I die, my mom will kill me!"

"Let's all calm down," Li'l Kimmy says, starting to pace around the desks. "Dying is pretty extreme. We just got left blindfolded in a small, claustrophobic room by a man who no one knows anything about or can get any background information on and who just said something really ominous."

She stops in her tracks. "Okay, it does seem pretty dire when I lay it out."

Edwin closes his eyes and thinks of his mother. He's trying not to devolve into a full-blown panic attack.

"But I don't think Onasander would put us in danger," Julie says softly. "He's a good guy."

"How can you be so sure?" Maureen says calmly, petting her own hair. "Like for real, what do we even know about him? This whole thing could be a huge scam. He could be anyone, with any motive."

"What motive, Maureen?" Li'l Kimmy asks, sounding almost, but not quite, angry.

"I'm just saying, he could be, like, evil. I mean, why would he trap us in this room?"

"Because we're supposed to solve the scavenger hunt," Edwin chimes in. "The puzzles. Remember?"

"I've never heard of a scavenger hunt that starts with being trapped, is all I'm saying. Seems weird. And fishy." Maureen sniffs.

"What about escape rooms?" Edwin challenges.

For once, Maureen does not have a snooty comeback. Because, after all, he's right.

"You know," Anton says, still sitting down and not looking up from his game, "in most video games, in these situations, people either band together to form an alliance and a leader emerges, or everyone turns on each other quickly and it gets violent."

"Are we, like, in a simulation?" Julie says, arms crossed.

Li'l Kimmy crosses the room to where Dilip is standing and slaps him.

"Hey! What was that for?!" Dilip yelps.

"Nope." Li'l Kimmy shrugs. "Looks like we're not in a simulation."

"Did you really have to test that?" Dilip says, touching his red cheek.

Li'l Kimmy shrugs. "You gotta do what you gotta do." Which isn't exactly an apology.

Edwin sits with his legs crossed, racking his brain for clues as to what could be going on. "Anton's right," he says finally. "Let's say we are in trouble. Historical precedent is for humans to behave in one of two ways when put in danger. Work together to form a team against opponents or self-destruct out of fear. Seems like we only have one viable option."

Julie looks at Edwin suspiciously. If there's anything middle school has taught her, it's to not trust her classmates. Especially not people who *enjoy* group projects. And work together with *these* people? Harold, who cheated on the assessment? And Maureen, who reminds Julie of her tormentors? Or even Li'l Kimmy, who's somehow louder than the entire timpani section of the New York Phil while still coming off as totally cool?

"Well, I for one am not trying to go all *Lord of the Flies* on your butts," Li'l Kimmy says, hands on her hips. "Aren't we more mature than that? Plus, what good would that do?"

Harold, meanwhile, is huffing in the corner. "What right does this man have to *trap* us?! Is he trying to kidnap me?! I need to speak to the management!" Harold should definitely be at some country club ordering staff about. He's got *nepo baby* written all over him.

Harold yanks out his phone and taps on it mercilessly, as if that will make the infinity symbol disappear. As he's engaging in his pointless behavior, he keeps shuffling slightly to his left. And suddenly, Julie sees why.

The walls of the small white room are shifting. Very, very slowly, almost imperceptibly. But the more she looks, the more she sees that they definitely *are* closing in. At first, she's scared to mention it. What if they don't believe her? Or worse, what if she's wrong? What if they laugh at her? Or think she's *annoying*? Over the years, she's learned to keep all her observations, her thoughts, her jokes, and her emotions to herself. But this seems, maybe, like it might be worth sharing. She waits for someone else to notice it, but they don't. Not even Harold, who keeps being forced to move sideways by a slowly moving wall.

"Uh, guys?" Julie says hesitantly.

They all look at her.

"I think the walls are closing in."

"What?" Maureen squawks. "Speak up!"

"The walls," Julie whispers.

"Julie, girl, you're gonna have to talk a little louder," Li'l Kimmy encourages her.

"THE WALLS ARE CLOSING IN ON US!" Julie finally yells.

Fourteen eyeballs widen and stare at her, then at the walls.

"Holy mother of Tony Hawk, she's right," Dilip says.

He runs to put his hands against the wall and feels it moving ever so slowly toward him. "Oh god! They're closing! We're going to get squished!"

"Death by drywall was *so* not how I was planning to go out," Maureen says.

"Okay, everybody, let's push!" Li'l Kimmy shouts.

Edwin, Li'l Kimmy, Maureen, Dilip, Julie, and Ting-Ting get up and brace themselves against the walls, pushing against them with all their strength. The walls just keep moving.

"Uh, you two want to give us a hand?" Li'l Kimmy says to Anton and Harold.

"I'm trying to make a call to my father's people," says Harold, still pressing the screen on his phone. "This is unacceptable. I'm not getting squished to death before we've even begun the first day of the seminars!"

"You know, I'm not sure there are going to *be* any seminars, Harold," Maureen says, leaning back against her wall to press her weight into it. "I think we're in for something a bit different than what we signed up for."

"Well, in that case, I need to speak to the person in charge! They are not delivering on what they advertised!"

"Anton?" Li'l Kimmy says, waving him over to help.

"I just lost!" he cries, and throws down his gaming device.

"You do realize," Li'l Kimmy says, "that you're gonna lose a life in *real life* if we get crushed, right? And not like, a video game life? You don't have multiple lives in real life. You can't just restart the game."

"How do you know? Have you ever died before?" Anton asks.

"Well . . . no." Li'l Kimmy frowns.

"Then you don't really know what you're talking about, do you?" He's already picked up the device again.

Li'l Kimmy lets out a frustrated, exasperated sigh. "Can we cut the philosophy crap until we're not in total mortal danger?!"

Anton just shrugs.

Li'l Kimmy cannot believe this. Who are these kids? Is she the only one that cares about saving their lives? She has a whole rap career ahead of her! She's not trying to die in a tiny room full of weirdos!

Julie notices that Edwin has been quiet for a while. She

finds him staring intently at one of the desks while pressing both hands into the wall. A little zing goes through her. This is a person who is forming a plan.

"Hey, Edwin," she says. "What are you thinking?"

Edwin tears his gaze from the circle-shaped desk.

"I think I have an idea."

Chapter Twelve

PUZZLED

"Look at the desks," Edwin says, climbing up on the circular desk in the center of the room.

They look around the small—and getting ever smaller—room. There are eight desks of different shapes and colors. Edwin Edgefield is not typically known for his physical solutions to problems. But his mind does work spatially as well as conceptually.

"I think they might fit together," he says. "And I think if we place them against the walls, they'll get pushed together and form a sort of barrier that will stop them from moving."

"They *are* really weird shapes," Maureen says. "I thought Onasander just had a horrible interior designer."

"So you think it's a puzzle?" Dilip asks. "Like maybe these are the puzzle pieces we're supposed to find?"

"Maybe!" Edwin says. "Or maybe not. I don't know. But I do think this will work. All of them except this circle need to be moved."

"Worth a try," Li'l Kimmy agrees.

"I like a good puzzle," Anton says hesitantly, putting down his video game at last.

In some ways, this makes Julie more nervous. If even Anton is getting freaked out enough to help, maybe they really are in trouble.

Edwin tries to direct everyone from his bird's-eye view. "The squiggle table needs to go over here, by the door."

"Okay," Maureen says. "Harold, get over here and help."

Harold just tells her to talk to the hand and looks the other way.

"Privileged kid thinks he can just do whatever he wants," Maureen mutters.

"Didn't you show up in a Tesla X?" Dilip says under his breath, so only Li'l Kimmy, moving toward an orange rhombus desk, can hear.

Li'l Kimmy has to hold in a laugh. She can smell a privileged private-school girl from a mile away, and Maureen's Chanel No. 5 isn't making that any harder. But Li'l Kimmy reminds herself not to judge. At least Maureen's pitching in. She can't be that bad.

Except the thing is . . .

"Um, Edwin?" Li'l Kimmy says, grunting as she tries to nudge her table from its spot. "These things are really heavy!"

"What?" Edwin asks.

The room keeps shrinking. Julie looks at the walls— they're definitely getting closer.

And closer.

Dilip strains under the weight of a purple trapezoidal table. "Yeah, man, they weigh a ton! Do you have any other ideas?"

Edwin shakes his head. He was sure he'd had it. Just place the tables where they fit.

That had to be the solution!

He closes his eyes and sees the tables fitting together and bracing against the walls. He knows this is the only way to stop the walls from crushing them.

"Ughhhh!" Maureen cries, trying to move the squiggle desk with Ting-Ting. "This is not happening!"

"We're going to get squished!" screams Julie.

Edwin takes deep breaths. He can see it—the tables lifting and arranging themselves together to create a barricade. He *knows* this is the solution. He can see it in his mind . . . the scalene triangle in an acute angle against the cone, the pyramid next to the kite . . . if he could only lift and place them in the right positions.

Suddenly, everyone is screaming.

Oh no!

The walls!

He's about to be squished!

But no. Now everyone is . . . laughing.

Huh?

Edwin opens his eyes.

Just as he had envisioned, the tables have arranged themselves neatly against each other, fitting piece to piece, creating a solid barrier against the walls.

"What happened?" he asks.

Julie can't believe it, even when she tells him. "The tables! They lifted themselves and locked into place! Did you do that?"

"ME?" Edwin yelps, still standing high over the room on the circle table. The other kids surround him on the floor, and the tables surround *them*, bracing the four walls. "No! How could I— I just—" He'd just *seen* it with his mind. Was it possible he'd moved them with his mind? No—that's impossible!

"Dude, it was you, one hundred percent," says Dilip. "You were holding your hands up and everything. Like a Jedi."

Maureen's eyes are narrowed at him. Ting-Ting is scribbling furiously in her notebook. Harold is . . . still tapping at his phone.

Dilip, Julie, and Li'l Kimmy high-five each other.

Anton sits back down and whips out his gaming console. "Looks like our leader has presented himself," he says, looking at the screen.

There's a moment of pause as everyone considers what Anton means, and then they look up to Edwin, standing above them. Edwin scratches his head and steps down sheepishly. All he did was put together some puzzle pieces in his mind. Could he have actually moved them? How can that be true?

Before anyone has a moment to consider what just happened, a new doorway appears. And don't get too English Lit on us: It's not a metaphorical doorway. It's a literal one. Smooth and silver and positioned halfway up the wall, just above the trapezoid-shaped desk.

"Where did that just come from?" Li'l Kimmy frowns. "That wasn't there before, right? I'm not imagining it?"

"No, it definitely wasn't," Julie says, joining Li'l Kimmy in frowning.

"Anyone ever heard of an Octagon project that can make a door appear out of thin air?" Li'l Kimmy says, looking at Edwin, Dilip, Julie, Maureen, and Ting-Ting. The other two are sort of useless at this point.

They all shrug.

None of them notice that the door has a slot in it until something comes shooting through it. Instinctively, they all recoil. The slot in the door disappears.

"What is that thing?" Dilip says, looking at the small silver shape that lands on the floor.

"Looks like we've got mail," Li'l Kimmy says.

She steps forward, gingerly, in case the silver thing explodes or something. It's an odd shape. Curved on one side, all jagged on the other. It has a line running through it that pulses with light.

"The puzzle piece," she says in wonder.

"I guess this means we passed the first test?" Julie says.

"Well, that, and we didn't get crushed to death," Dilip adds.

"Do we touch it?" Maureen asks.

"I think we have to. . . . I think we're going to need it," Edwin says.

Li'l Kimmy picks things up off the sidewalk all the time in LA, and the chance of something being radioactive is probably higher there. She snatches the thing off the floor. It's about the size of her palm and extremely light.

"Who wants to be the keeper of the puzzle pieces?" she asks the group.

"Dilip has the most pockets," Julie notes.

"Fair," Dilip says diplomatically. His board shorts have cargo-style pockets on them. "They have zippers, too," he says. "Should be safe in here, just like my snacks."

"Oh goodie." Maureen rolls her eyes. "Let's just hope you don't get Cheeto dust on the puzzle piece."

Dilip ignores her, though how did she know he has Cheetos in there? Hot Cheetos, to be precise. He puts the puzzle piece in a right-side pocket and zips it in for safekeeping. First puzzle piece: acquired. Now there's the matter of the mysterious silver door to attend to.

"What's on the other side?" Dilip asks, sitting lightly on the desk in front of it.

"Could be something good . . ." Li'l Kimmy ventures, taking a slow step closer.

"Or could be something very bad." Maureen grimaces.

"So it's like Schrödinger's cat," Julie says, laughing quietly to herself.

"What's that?" Maureen turns around.

Julie's sitting on the floor, re-braiding her hair. She looks up at Maureen. "Schrödinger's cat. You know, the theoretical experiment? Scientists would put a cat in a box with a flask of poison that's rigged so there's an equal chance it might explode and kill the cat and it might not. The scientists running the experiment would have no way of knowing whether the cat was dead or alive while it was in the box."

"Right!" Edwin says. "So in the Copenhagen interpretation of quantum mechanics, after a while, you can assume that the cat is both alive *and* dead!"

"Way to steal a girl's thunder, Edwin," Li'l Kimmy says, shaking her head.

"Oh." Edwin's chest deflates like a week-old birthday balloon. "Sorry, Julie. I just got excited. I don't usually know people who reference Schrödinger's cat."

Julie smiles at Edwin. Having someone around who appreciates her bringing up a theory of quantum mechanics makes up for it.

"It's cool," she says. "I was just saying, until we open the door, we can assume that there's both something good and something bad beyond it."

They consider the door, imagining what might be behind it. Whether Onasander is benevolent like they thought, or whether they've been tricked into some bizarre and dangerous test, there's no other choice. The only way out is through.

Chapter Thirteen

A STRANGE EQUATION

"**D**o you think we should open it?" Julie whispers.

"I guess we can try?" Dilip ventures. He stands up on the desk next to the door and braces himself. "Let's just hope there's not a dead cat lying behind this door, right?" he says, trying to lighten the mood.

"I think that would be a best-case scenario at this point," Julie sighs.

Dilip tries the handle. It doesn't move. The moment he touches it, though, the entire door emits a phosphorescent glow and symbols appear.

"Whoa!" says Li'l Kimmy. "Epic!"

Dilip backs up in surprise. His fingers have left a silvery glowing smudge on the door handle.

"What is that, some kind of ancient language?" he asks, squinting at the strange numeric symbols and numbers now pulsing with silver light.

"It looks like a math problem to me," Li'l Kimmy says.

Ting-Ting stares intently at the math problem, takes out her notebook, and starts scribbling furiously.

"You know how to solve this, Ting-Ting?" Li'l Kimmy asks.

Ting-Ting shrugs. "Every time I see a math problem, I feel the need to write it down. You never know when you'll be tested."

"We're being tested right now, Ting-Ting," Maureen says. *"Obviously."*

This statement makes Ting-Ting look nauseous.

Edwin can relate. He feels his anxiety build. If they don't solve the math problem, if they don't clear these obstacles, what happens? Do they get kicked out of the Octagon Institute? Or is it something worse? Who is Onasander Octagon, anyway? Is this the ultimate gaslighting? But why gaslight eight sixth-graders?

"Well," Dilip starts, "I'm no help on this one. Math is not my thing."

"I'm in," Li'l Kimmy offers. "I know it's a total stereotype that Asians are good at math." She smirks. "But in this case, it's true."

"Julie?" Edwin asks.

"Music is basically math," Julie says. "I could try?" She's actually an A+ student in math and is taking college-level calculus, but she knows better than to show off.

"Don't look at me," Maureen says, whipping out a nail file and going to work on her thumbnail. "If you want to compound interest, I'm your girl, but I don't even know what half of that means."

Ting-Ting shivers, squinting at the problem fearfully. And no one bothers with Harold or Anton.

Edwin takes a step toward the door and studies the problem. "I think I can get us to this point." He scribbles some numbers on the door with his fingertip and they stay, pulsing like the rest of the numbers. "But I'm not sure what to do about this variable."

"Yes! You suck, ninja dude!" shouts Anton.

Julie pipes up at the same time as Anton, but Li'l Kimmy and Edwin don't seem to hear her. She tries to chime in again, but it comes out even softer this time. Not a head turns.

Li'l Kimmy studies Edwin's calculations and closes her eyes. She enters a sort of trance state, the same one that allowed her to pass the OVAEO. It's the same kind of zone her favorite rappers get into when they hit a particularly difficult flow. Some deeper part of the brain takes over. While math is not her favorite (she's more of a humanities girl—English Lit, Language Arts, that kind of thing), she *is* good at it. She can follow logic. Logic is structure, like rap. She thinks she hears someone say something, but she can't let her concentration break.

"Maybe this would work?" she asks, conferring with Edwin.

He nods. "Yes! *Yes!* I can't believe I missed that."

"And what about this?" Li'l Kimmy adds, drawing more equations on the board. "If we do that plus x, that should solve y, right?"

Julie wants to speak up. It's obvious to her what they're missing in trying to do all these complex complications. It's enough to make her downright laugh, if she weren't dying inside from being so overlooked. She tries again to comment, but Edwin speaks over her, agreeing with what Li'l Kimmy has done. She's starting to get fed up, starting to be reminded of her classmates back home. Well, if they don't want to listen to what she has to say, fine.

"Yeah, I think we did it," he says with quiet elation. He's never had friends to solve math problems with before! "Don't you think?"

Edwin doesn't want to presume to be their leader, or tell people what to do. But too little, too late, Edwin. He may have Albert Einstein–level intelligence, but he's not exactly Brené Brown–level emotionally intelligent.

"So what," Maureen pipes up, "if you guys get the question right, you think the door will open for us? And we'll go on to the next test?"

"Or maybe the room will blow up," Julie ventures. She's not bitter no one listened to her. Nope, not at all.

"Lighten up, Jules," Li'l Kimmy says. "Maybe the room will blow up . . . with confetti!"

Edwin laughs. "Dilip, you want to do the honors?"

Dilip steps forward and once again places his hand on the door handle. He turns around in glee. "Not locked!"

He carefully pulls open the door, and the six of them hold their breath in anticipation of what lies on the other side. A trap? A treat?

Instead, there's nothing. Literally nothing.

"Whoo! Beat another level!" shouts Anton.

The door opens to a mirror that doesn't hold their reflections, and then the seven of them—not including Harold—are pulled with an unbelievably powerful force, as if invisible hands are yanking them, into the nothingness.

"GAH!" they scream.

They float, feet dangling in the air, weightless, in a pitch black the likes of which they've never seen before. Because you can't even *see* it. It's not darkness, it's nothing. It's a void. Julie turns around, wondering if she's the only one here. She can't see anyone at all! Is she alone?

"Hello?" she calls out, and there's no echo. The sound of her voice seems to dissolve into nothingness as soon as it leaves her mouth.

"Where are we?" Dilip's voice says, sounding very, very far away.

"Oh my god!" Maureen's voice screeches in the darkness. "I so did not sign up for this!"

"Is everyone here?" Julie asks, and Edwin and Li'l Kimmy say hi in response, Anton just grunts, and Ting-Ting coughs.

Julie turns around from her floating position and sees a square of bright white light in the distance. She squints, and she can just make out shapes and colors in the center of the white light. It's the doorway to the waiting room!

In this void they're in, there's no floor that anyone can see, no ceiling, nothing to grip to get your bearings. Just an endless, starless, formless black.

It's a bizarre, uncanny sensation, floating in nothingness. Julie's eyes lose focus, as there's nothing for them to grab onto. But even if they adjusted to the dark, this is a psychedelic trip of total emptiness.

Li'l Kimmy's voice cuts through the darkness. "Wait a second," she says. "You guys . . . don't you think we might be . . . in a black hole?"

There's a collective gasp. A black hole? They're inside a black hole?!

"Actually, you guys," Julie chimes in softly, as if she's hesitant to correct anyone but feels it's her duty, "it can't be a black hole. According to quantum physics, if we were this close to a black hole, we'd all be instantly crushed."

"Really?" Li'l Kimmy asks.

"I'm kind of obsessed with black holes," Julie says, shrugging, though no one can see the shrug.

"Black holes and quantum physics and violins. Cool," Li'l Kimmy's voice says.

"You really think that's cool?" Julie whispers, wary that she's being mocked.

"Totally dope," Li'l Kimmy says.

Julie smiles. Thank goodness no one can see her smile. Maybe they weren't ignoring her on purpose.

"Um, you guys, I think we got the answer wrong," says Li'l Kimmy. "We messed up."

"Messed up how?" Dilip's voice calls from far away.

"Dilip, where are you?" Li'l Kimmy says. "You sound so far!"

"Sorry," Dilip says, his voice getting progressively louder. "I figured out while you guys were talking that you can sort of ride the flotation of the nothingness around. Almost like surfing."

"Dilip," Li'l Kimmy says, laughing, "I don't know you that well, but I can already tell that only you would immediately figure out how to surf the darkness."

"What do you mean you guys messed up?" Ting-Ting says. "What did you do? How did you mess this up for us?!"

"Ting-Ting, chill," Li'l Kimmy says. "You sound stressed."

"WE'RE IN THE MIDDLE OF A BLACK HOLE

OF COURSE I'M STRESSED!" Ting-Ting yells at hyper speed.

"It's not a black hole," Julie says again, quietly.

Edwin, meanwhile, is recalculating the solution in his mind. He has a photographic memory and can see every single step they took clearly. He shakes his head.

"No way. I know we got it right," Edwin says, hackles rising. He always gets math problems right. Always. If he doesn't have that, what does he have? "Maybe we just need to figure out how to get out of here."

Julie takes a deep breath. "Maybe the only way to get out of here is to admit we were wrong," she says gently, as if she can sense Edwin's prickliness about the matter.

As soon as she says it, as quickly as they were yanked into the nothingness, they're spat back out.

The seven of them cough and sputter on their hands and knees on the bright white floor of the waiting room.

Harold looks up from his phone and raises an eyebrow.

They ignore him. He wasn't much help before, and he won't be much help now. Seriously, how is Harold still in this story?

The silver door closes behind them, shutting them off from the black void. They hear it click and lock.

"Oh," says Edwin, dumbfounded. He fights a sick feeling in his stomach. "I guess we *were* wrong."

And somehow it doesn't kill him to say this out loud. It hurts, but it doesn't kill him.

"It's all right. We can just try again," says Li'l Kimmy. "Edwin?"

He still feels ill, but he nods. "Let's do it. Can't be worse than falling into a void."

Chapter Fourteen

DIVISION AND DIVISIONS

"So, are we going to talk about the fact that we were just floating in space, or what?" Ting-Ting says. "Like, how did that just happen?!"

No one answers her. The only sound is Harold still furiously tapping away on his phone screen.

"If I never saw this room again, I would be very happy," Anton mutters.

"Anton, you aren't even seeing this room. You're in some other world," Maureen says, kicking his game console out of his hands.

"Hey! Watch it!" He scrambles to pick it back up. "I almost beat this boss!"

"I think we might have an *actual* boss on our hands," Julie says sourly. She can't believe she had actually been looking forward to this weekend. To maybe, possibly (unrealistically?) making friends her own age. Because Mathilde from the string section can be very sweet and all, but what kind of twelve-year-old kid from the New York suburbs has a forty-seven-year-old, native French–speaking BFF? But Onasander Octagon is certainly not turning out to be who she thought he was. First, they were almost squished to death, then they were sent into a void? He's got to be some kind of villain, right?

She turns her attention back to Li'l Kimmy and Edwin at the door. Neither of them have asked for her help, even after she tried telling them, multiple times, what she thought. Still, even after getting it wrong, they haven't asked. What hubris!

Edwin is back at the drawing board, literally, running his hand over his cropped hair in frustration. Where did they go wrong? What part of his calculation was incorrect? Is he a total failure? What if he really isn't that smart? What if, his whole life, he's just been in situations that have been really easy, and he never knew it? He wipes the door, deciding to start from scratch. With math problems, sometimes it's so difficult to figure out where you went wrong that it's easier just to start from the beginning.

He sighs. "What about this?" he asks Li'l Kimmy.

"Are you sure you passed the OVAEO, Edwin?" Ting-Ting says. "You don't seem very good at this."

"Way harsh, Ting-Ting," Li'l Kimmy says. "I don't see you solving the problem."

Ting-Ting pulls her knees up under her chin and opens her notebook.

"I'm boooored," Maureen says, lying flat on the rhombus desk. "Can't you guys hurry up and fix your answer?"

Dilip can sense Li'l Kimmy's *Lord of the Flies* prophecy coming true. He decides to distract everyone with something he was thinking about while in the void.

"Have you guys ever heard of Daedalus's labyrinth?" he says.

"What's that got to do with anything, Dilip?" Maureen yawns.

"Well, that void thing was pretty weird, right?"

"You could say that again," Li'l Kimmy says with a laugh, turning away from the door.

"So I was just thinking about, like, where are we? Like, what is this Octagon Valley place?"

"You mean how could there be a mysterious endless void inside a building?" Maureen asks.

"Right. And I mean, are we expecting that when the door opens again, after they solve the problem, that somewhere new will be revealed? That will be different than the void?" Dilip asks.

"*Is* that what we're thinking?" Ting-Ting says, pen poised over her notebook.

"So, what if we're in a labyrinth of some kind? Or maybe *maze* is a better term for it. You know those tall hedge mazes in old movies?"

They all nod, picturing tall green hedges forming zig-zag patterns and right angles.

"I think we might be in some sort of magical maze," Dilip concludes.

The seven of them consider this. A maze? A *magical* maze? Could the Octagon Valley Institute compound be a magical mystery maze?

"Back in the void, when I was surfing around, I touched what felt like a wall," Dilip adds.

"A wall?" Ting-Ting squints, jotting this down without even looking at the notebook. "In the *void*. That would make it not a void." She looks around at the others uncertainly. "Right?"

"Yeah, a wall. Like, the wall of the building. So even though it felt like a total void, I think maybe we were still inside a room in Octagon Valley."

Ting-Ting diligently writes this down.

"How could that be possible?" Anton asks, not lifting his eyes from his game. "I mean, I see how it could be possible in a video game, but IRL?"

"Magic?" Dilip posits.

"Do we believe in magic?" Julie asks.

All six of them, minus Edwin, who is recalculating the math problem, shake their heads.

"Jeez, we are some jaded middle schoolers," Li'l Kimmy announces.

"Magic doesn't exist," Edwin agrees. "It's just science.

'Any sufficiently advanced technology is indistinguishable from magic.'"

"Arthur C. Clarke," Anton murmurs, looking up. It's the first time Anton has looked anyone in the eye.

"Exactly."

"Okay, so everything in this place must be based on science of some kind," Julie says. "A very advanced kind of science that could mimic the feeling of being in a black hole, without the consequences."

"What on earth kind of science could that be?" Ting-Ting says, writing furiously.

"Maybe it's not science from this Earth," Maureen says softly.

Li'l Kimmy can barely hear what she said, but she sees a strange, sly expression form on Maureen's face. "What did you say, Maureen?" she asks. But Maureen doesn't answer.

Edwin is still staring at the board, scratching his head. This is getting ridiculous.

"Edwin?" Julie asks.

He turns around quickly.

"Do you have any ideas, Julie?" he asks her.

Hmm. Maybe he really just didn't hear her earlier and wasn't ignoring her.

"I do, actually. I tried telling you guys before we got sucked into the void, but you didn't listen."

"We didn't?" Li'l Kimmy says, looking slightly ashamed.

"Or maybe you just didn't hear me."

Edwin feels embarrassment creep up the back of his skull. "Gosh, I'm sorry, Julie. We were so wrapped up in the puzzle."

"What I was trying to tell you is that the equation is totally simple." Julie shrugs.

Simple?! Li'l Kimmy and Edwin look at each other in astonishment. They've been busting their brains over this equation, and she's saying it's simple?

"Look." Julie walks over to the silver board. She points at the bottom corner of the equation. In silver shimmery letters, there it is. $x(0)$. X times zero. Times nothing. Multiply by zero. So, of course, the answer is . . .

"Zero." Edwin stares in awe. He writes the answer on the board.

"I tried to tell you," Julie mutters. But, she realizes, she also didn't quite try hard enough. Until now. She has to remember that: Be a little louder. She can speak up. They won't find her annoying. (Maybe.)

"You know," Anton chimes in, eyes still locked on his video game, "good leaders actually listen to the people on their team."

What was that? Anton Chesky, voice of reason?

For once, Julie agrees with him. "That is how I try to be as a conductor," she mumbles.

"What was that, Julie?" Li'l Kimmy asks.

Julie takes a breath. *Louder.* "I said, that's how I try to be as a conductor. For my orchestra. Listen to the people on my team."

"I'm sorry, Julie," Edwin says. "I feel like such a jerk."

"You don't have to feel like a jerk." She meets his eyes. "Just remember to check in with your team."

"So that means we're a team?" Li'l Kimmy grins.

"A team that solved the equation." Julie smiles back.

"Are you sure?" Ting-Ting says a little bitterly, though she's done zip to help the situation. "I do not want to end up in a black hole again."

"It wasn't a black hole!" Dilip, Julie, and Li'l Kimmy all say at the same time, then burst out laughing.

"Guys, the door?" Maureen says, bringing them back to Earth.

"Try the handle," says Edwin.

Dilip runs over to the door and tries it. "Unlocked. It . . . worked?"

"Okay," says Edwin. "Let's open it. Let's see where it goes."

The seven of them huddle behind him. One of them is missing.

"Harold, get off your phone and get over here," Li'l Kimmy calls over her shoulder. She doesn't exactly love the guy, but it seems cruel to leave him all alone. Unless, of course, what's behind the door now is actually *worse* than the black hole, in which case, it might be more merciful to leave him behind.

"I'm sure any minute I'm going to get service again," Harold says.

"Didn't you hear Onasander? Phones don't work in here!" Edwin says. "Get up, Harold, come on, we have to go."

"Whatever, Edwin. I didn't even want to be here in the first place. My dad made me come. He said Postmans are always chosen! I don't want to do another round of stupid tests."

"Harold, if you don't come with us, we don't know what will happen to you!" Li'l Kimmy says.

"I'll be fine. I have my phone, that's all I need. I'll call my dad's bodyguards to come get me as soon as the service is back up and running."

Edwin shakes his head in disbelief. What isn't Harold getting? There's no one coming to save them.

"Forget it, guys," Maureen says to the group. "What are we going to do, wait around all day trying to convince him? This whole thing probably has a time limit. What if the walls start moving again?"

They look at each other. She's not wrong.

"I just feel weird about leaving him in here," Li'l Kimmy says. "Didn't Octagon say something about working together?"

"I haven't been paying much attention this whole time,"

says Anton, "but even I can tell you that Harold has zero interest in working together."

"Yeah. Besides, it's Harold's decision. Ever heard of free will?" Maureen quips.

Li'l Kimmy sighs, trying not to lose her cool. "Yes, I've heard of free will. Ever heard of compassion?"

"Tick, tock! Tick, tock!" Maureen says.

"Fine! Harold, this is your last chance," Li'l Kimmy says. "Are you coming, or what?"

"Well, where does the door lead to?" he asks.

"We don't know. That's kind of the whole point."

Harold just frowns, and stares at his phone screen.

"Let's *go*," Maureen says.

"We leave him?" asks Li'l Kimmy.

"We leave him." Julie nods. Dilip reluctantly agrees as well. Anton kills another ninja. Ting-Ting jots it all down in her notebook.

It's settled.

Bye, Harold! Can't believe you made it this far! Swore you'd be gone by Chapter Two!

Edwin takes a breath. "Dilip, open the door."

Chapter Fifteen

SOOTHING THE SAVAGE BEAST

"**W**hy does Dilip always get to open the door?" Maureen sniffs as Dilip pulls on the handle. Before anyone can answer, a similar feeling grips the seven of them and pulls them through the doorway with a *swoosh*. *Splash!*

Julie is suddenly submerged. She shoves herself up and gasps for air, then sees the others doing the same. They've landed in the middle of a body of water, and though it's fairly deep, she can stand up and touch the bottom if she goes on her very tiptoes. She catches her breath and sees that there's land on either side of the water. They've landed, somehow, some way, in a river.

She looks backward just in time to see the silver door

they came through close. *In midair.* The door dims, then becomes translucent until it disappears completely, leaving no trace it was ever there. Now it's just a bright blue sky.

"Edwin," Ting-Ting says between gasps, "I think you guys messed up again. And I lost my notebook!"

"No way," he says with a conviction that is new to him. "I *know* we got it right this time."

"And remember," Dilip says, treading water, "it wasn't just Edwin who solved that. I guess this is the next obstacle?"

In front of Dilip, something floats up from the bottom of the river. Silver, shiny.

"Hey, the next puzzle piece!" Dilip exclaims, grabbing it and waving it for them all to see.

"Amazing!" Li'l Kimmy chimes in. "So we did get it right!"

"Did Harold get swept up with us?" Maureen says, paddling around in the river and counting all the heads. There's Ting-Ting, frowning and breathing heavily. There's Dilip, diving underwater and pushing off the bottom of the river to pop up in a big burst of a jump. There's Li'l Kimmy, floating leisurely on her back. There's Anton, unmoving except to hold his game console above his head to make sure it doesn't get any more water on it. There's Julie, humming and looking around, taking in the environment. And there's Edwin, struggling to keep his head above water and trying to absorb everything in sight.

But no Harold. Thankfully, we said goodbye to him in the last chapter!

"I guess he's still in the other room," Li'l Kimmy says.

"You think he's okay?" Ting-Ting asks nervously. "What's gonna happen to him?"

No one answers. Are they all in real danger? What does Onasander Octagon want from them? And what does this river have to do with it?

"Oh gosh, oh gosh," Ting-Ting cries. "Is Harold going to die?"

Wait. Is this what Ting-Ting is like without her notebook? Julie can't decide whether she likes clinical Ting-Ting or emotional Ting-Ting.

"Where are we?" Anton says, finally forced to look at something other than his game.

The river stretches endlessly in front of them like a dark green snake. On either side of the riverbed, there are lush tropical forests. A flock of rainbow-colored parrots flutter out from the treetops. And is that a spotted leopard?

"Are we in the Amazon rainforest?" Dilip asks. "And, like, the Amazon River? Kinda looks like it."

The others nod, remembering various biology classes, geography classes, *National Geographic* issues, and Discovery Channel shows.

"But are we *actually* in the Amazon rainforest?" Li'l Kimmy asks. "Like, did we get teleported here somehow?"

"That would be sick," Anton adds.

"I don't think that's scientifically possible quite yet," Edwin says. "Unless Onasander is working with something that's far beyond anything anyone knows about."

"He is always very cryptic about his research in his Octo Talks," Julie notes.

"You watch those too?" Edwin smiles.

"Totally. They got me through some rough nights," she says, grinning. But then she catches herself. She feels odd, bonding.

"Me too!" Edwin replies excitedly.

Julie smiles but doesn't know what else to say. She's far more comfortable observing than participating. So Edwin is left hanging in excitement alone.

"What about a hologram?" Li'l Kimmy suggests, swimming toward the shore at the edge of the river, assuming the others will follow. "Could this all be a hologram?"

"I feel pretty wet," Dilip says, swimming to catch up with Li'l Kimmy. "Are holograms that advanced, that you can feel sensations in them?"

"Maybe we're in a virtual reality," Maureen says. She swims forward to catch up with Dilip and Li'l Kimmy.

"I don't remember putting on a headset, though," Anton responds. "And there's no virtual reality on the market where you can feel texture."

Stunned by the impossibility of dropping into the middle of the Amazon, the seven of them make their way toward the riverbank, taking in the shocking beauty of the scenery around them.

"The rainforest is so beautiful," Li'l Kimmy says dreamily.

"My mother is going to kill me when she finds out I lost my notebook!" Ting-Ting cries.

"There's an incredible amount of biodiversity here, you know," Edwin says. "There are forty thousand plant species. Over four hundred and thirty mammal species!"

The trees rustle with a breeze, and colorful birds continue to flit from perch to perch. They all admire it, except for Julie. Wildlife really freaks her out. It has ever since she was a kid. She tries to ignore the others oohing and aahing at the creatures on the shore. She's happy to stay in the water for a while longer if it means staying away from the animals.

The current is strong, rushing around them. It makes it a little hard to hear. Even though the riverbank isn't so far, it's surprisingly difficult to move forward. The waves seem to be picking up.

"Anton! What are you doing?!" Dilip points.

Anton is still holding his video game console above the water, trying to walk through the rushing river rather than swim.

"Anton, drop the game and swim for it! Come on!" Li'l Kimmy screams. "You're going to drown!"

"I can't!" Anton yells back.

"You have to! It's just a game!"

"I'm not talking about the game. I can't swim!"

Suddenly Anton is struggling against the current. Water fills his mouth, and he spits it out, choking.

"What did you say?" Dilip asks over the rush of the water.

"I! CAN'T! SWIM!" Anton sputters.

And just like that, he gets knocked over by a wave, and his head and gaming device both go under.

"Anton!" Li'l Kimmy shouts.

Dilip swims with full force toward the spot where Anton disappeared. He dives under and comes back up seconds later, Anton on his back.

"Dilip, can you swim like that?" Li'l Kimmy yells to him.

"Not sure, never tried!" Dilip yells back. "But I've seen lifeguards do it! How hard can it be?"

They slowly eke their way toward the shore, the current still pushing at them hard. Thanks to Anton's added weight, Dilip drags far behind the rest of them. Edwin's up ahead rambling on about the variety of birds by the river. He's interrupted by Dilip's scream.

"Fish! Fish!" Dilip screams.

"Yes, three thousand fish species!" Edwin confirms. He turns around in the water and notices, for the first time, that Dilip is carrying Anton.

"No, Edwin. *Fish with teeth!*"

Edwin frowns and looks down into the water where Dilip is pointing. Hovering there, between them, is a school of piranhas, all baring their razor-sharp teeth.

GAH!

"RUN!" Dilip yells.

"We can't run!" Maureen squeals. "We're in water!"

"Then swim!"

Julie isn't sure that swimming will make much of a difference. After all, piranhas are aquatic creatures, and they're sure to outswim even the fastest of middle schoolers.

"Ouch!" Dilip yells. "It bit me! One of these bit me!"

He tries to kick a piranha, but it just bites his foot. With Anton on his back, Dilip's super slow and a prime target.

The school of razor-sharp-toothed fish swarms closer. If they don't do something soon, they're all going to be fish food.

Do something! Julie thinks. She is closest to the edge of the river now, as Edwin has swum back toward Dilip and Anton. She can stand again. *This can't be how it ends.*

Above her, Julie hears birdsong. It calms her instantly. Music. Music! People have always told her that she has an unnatural musical gift. Unnatural as in no kid should be able to do what she does with music. But really, no adult can either. Which is why she became a conductor. When she conducts, it doesn't feel like she's giving her musicians a rhythm to follow. It's much more than that. It's like she's controlling them. Like she's *playing* them, just like they're playing their instruments. Not that she would ever admit it out loud.

She never lets herself think about that one night. It confuses her too much. Sometimes, she pretends that she dreamed the whole thing, just to make it easier to understand. But she knows that she didn't dream it. It happened years ago. She was alone at a family friend's lake house. All the parents were inside, and there she was, by the lake. It was evening. There were fireflies buzzing all around her. There were mosquitoes too. Music poured out of the kitchen windows as her parents passed around wine and chopped vegetables for dinner.

The music is so nice, she remembers thinking. She was probably only five years old then. The whole scene was so lovely, except for the mosquitoes. She remembers thinking that if only she could get rid of all the mosquitoes, if they would clump together and drown in the lake, then her night would be perfect. Oh, and if the fireflies all danced together, swaying in tune to the music, how lovely would that be? Then the night would be perfect. And then she began to hum, imagining all of this happening. She listened to the music, and hummed, and then she heard a buzzing. A loud buzzing—almost a screeching. Little bugs flew through the air, all drawn to the same source. Above the lake, hundreds of mosquitoes buzzed together to form one giant ball in the air, a bloodsucking, squeaky mass. Then they plunged into the lake, just like that. All the mosquitoes drowned. Meanwhile, all the fireflies swayed to the beat.

She knew that she had done it. She had killed all the mosquitos with her music! And made the fireflies dance! But how could she ever explain it? She had no proof she had done it, and for years she had buried the memory deep. It frightened her that she could do something like that. Something so violent. She'll never forget all the mosquitoes drowning en masse. If she could do that, what else could she do?

Maybe this is why animals scare her so much. Ever since that moment, Julie has wanted to stay away from them as much as she can. She can't bear accidentally harming something just by thinking about it. It's terrifying. And people already think she's enough of a freak. *Voted "Most Annoying."* *House TP-ed by the entire class. Booed to her face.* No middle schooler has ever been so loathed.

And why?

Just because she is different? Smarter? *Is* she annoying?

Or worse—is she dangerous?

All of this flits through her mind in an instant. Could her worst fear, the thing she's hidden from herself for years, possibly work in a scenario like this? Was it even real? She listens intently to the birdsong as she and the six other "winners" of the Octagon Valley Assessment for the Extra-Ordinary swim for their lives. There's no choice.

She has to try. Julie starts singing, mimicking the tune of the birds in the trees. The current ebbs as she watches the piranhas and plants her feet on the riverbed, raising her hands like she would above her orchestra.

"Julie!" Dilip cries. "What are you doing?! You're going to get eaten! Keep swimming!"

But she knows what she has to do, and she'll risk it if it means that they won't all get eaten alive. This better work! She begins to use the song of the birds, singing along, to tap into the piranhas. Is she out of her mind? She can't actually *control* their minds, can she? It must have been a fluke memory. She's probably just a really good conductor. But wait . . . no piranhas are biting her. In fact, they're just floating motionlessly. They look almost . . . hypnotized?

"Quick, everyone, swim to the edge of the river!" she instructs over her shoulder.

Maureen pokes at a floating piranha. It doesn't react. "Whoa."

The others swim for it with bewildered expressions on their faces. Edwin and Li'l Kimmy grab one of Anton's arms as Dilip grabs the other, and they carry him forward as they swim. Maureen and Ting-Ting follow behind. They crawl up onto the riverbank, and once they're all up there, Julie drops her hands from conducting position and clambers toward shore.

As soon as she stops, the piranhas start swimming after her, but she's gotten enough of a head start that when Edwin and Li'l Kimmy pull her up onto dry land, she leaves the piranhas gnashing hungrily in her wake.

Chapter Sixteen

IT'S ALL GREEK TO ME

"Julie, what was that?" Dilip asks. "I mean, I can't even understand what I saw."

"Seriously, Julie!" Li'l Kimmy exclaims. "How did you do that?"

The seven of them shake water off their clothes, which are totally soaked down to their dripping sneakers, and wring out their hair. On the shoreline, Julie spots it. A third puzzle piece. She picks it up and tosses it to Dilip to put in his pocket.

"I'm not really sure," Julie admits. It's the truth, though she feels tingly all over, the adrenaline still rushing through her. "I don't even know what I did, really. Just conducted them, I guess. I told them to leave us alone."

Li'l Kimmy side-eyes Julie. She feels like Julie knows

more than she's letting on. There's no way piranhas can be *conducted* into peacefulness. Unless it's some weird evolutionary thing she doesn't know about. Something else is going on here; she's just not sure what, exactly. And didn't Edwin lift all those heavy desks with his mind as well?

"Uh, thanks for saving me, Dilip," Anton says. "I mean, all of you."

Dilip tears one of the sleeves off his long-sleeved T-shirt and ties it around his bleeding ankle. "Anytime."

They start walking along the shoreline.

"Did you know that if there were four hundred piranhas that attacked you, it would only take them five minutes to turn you into a skeleton?" Edwin says casually. When he's nervous, he tends to rely on facts and figures. It's perhaps not his most well-timed trait.

The other six stop in their tracks, horrified.

"Sorry," he says.

"At least you didn't tell us until we got out of the water," Li'l Kimmy says, slapping Edwin on the back.

"So it appears that even when we solve the puzzles correctly, we still face death," Edwin says. Because they got a puzzle piece for solving the puzzle on the door, but that just dropped them in a river with flesh-eating piranhas.

"But is it *real* death?" Li'l Kimmy asks. "Or is it just part of the obstacle course?"

"I feel like Onasander wouldn't put us in real danger," Edwin says.

"Felt pretty real to me," Dilip says, lifting his ankle.

Ting-Ting looks a tad green.

"But what do we really know about this Onasander guy, anyway?" Anton asks. Now that his device is gone, he seems to be dialed in.

"Yeah, what if he's trying to get rid of us?" Li'l Kimmy suggests.

"Get rid of us? Why would he want to do that?" Ting-Ting shivers.

"I don't know, because he's an evil villain?"

Edwin doesn't want to hear it. He doesn't want to stop believing in Onasander. He figures that while he's here in the Amazon, or at least some version of the Amazon, he may as well indulge his curiosity. He breaks off from the others, who are all walking along the river, and goes toward the trees. He just wants to take a peek deeper inside the jungle and see if there are any rare creatures in there. But as he takes a step in, he bumps against something. It feels like a wall. A wall? It doesn't look like a wall. When standing a few feet away, it looks just like a three-dimensional jungle. He reaches out. Midair, his hand hits something. He runs his hands along the smooth surface, his brain not fully processing what's going on.

"Hey, you guys, come here!" he calls.

The others stop talking and walk over to join him.

"What's up?" asks Dilip.

"I think there's a wall here," he says.

"A wall?" Anton says, and reaches forward. His knuckles hit something, and then he flattens his hand against it. "Cool! So we're in a simulation after all?"

"I'm not quite sure *simulation* is the right word . . ." says Edwin. "But we're definitely not in the actual Amazon."

"It's like what Dilip said!" Li'l Kimmy says brightly. "We're in a maze. We're in Onasander's maze, inside Octagon Valley!"

Bravo! Looks like our seven are on the right track after all.

"So each door we find leads us to a different room of the maze?" Ting-Ting asks. Her fingers twitch. She wishes she could take notes.

"I think so, Ting-Ting," Li'l Kimmy says.

"All right, so we have to find a door, then," Maureen asserts.

Edwin thinks that if there were an observer watching them from on high, perhaps sitting in a box somewhere or peering through a window in the ceiling, they would see a rather strange sight. Seven middle schoolers spread out in a line, patting what looks like thin air but is really a wall, along the edge of a jungle. Then he wonders if there *is* an observer. Onasander? Is he watching them?

"Eureka!" Dilip shouts.

"I think that only applies when you spontaneously have an epiphany," Maureen quips.

"What would you call this if not an epiphany?" Dilip smirks at her, revealing the outline of a door on a tree trunk.

"Finding something isn't an epiphany, Dilip," she sneers.

"Well, it certainly felt like one, Maureen." He rolls his eyes at her.

The surfer and the prep-school diva look at each other as if they're about to come to blows.

"Okay, okay, truce," Li'l Kimmy interjects. "This is great, Dilip."

Edwin approaches the door, checking for more math problems. There are none, and he's a little disappointed. It was fun solving the equation with Julie and Li'l Kimmy. Even if he did sort of take over before Julie pointed out his tendency to take center stage. But hey, he came here to learn, didn't he? And he's learning about being a teammate. That part, at least, lived up to his hopes for the weekend.

"Hey, what's this?" Julie says, kneeling next to the door. "It looks like some strange code."

Written on the trunk is a sequence of text made up of three languages. Edwin guesses that the text in each language is likely saying the same thing.

"It's like the Rosetta Stone," Ting-Ting says in an awed voice.

"Remind me—what's that again?" Dilip asks.

"It's how the modern world was able to translate ancient Egyptian hieroglyphs," Ting-Ting says. "There were three versions of the same text written on an ancient stone. One in Egyptian hieroglyphs, one in Demotic script, and one in Greek script. No one knew anything about how to read the hieroglyphs, but by using the Greek translation, they deciphered it."

"That's incredible!" Julie says, running her hands over the three scripts on the tree trunk. It feels like smooth wood with etched indentations. "So, this is like some sort of version of the Rosetta Stone?"

"I'm guessing it uses the same principles of translation." Ting-Ting shrugs.

"All right, then, so all we have to do is translate these three languages. And the first thing we have to do is figure out what they are," Li'l Kimmy jokes. "Easy."

The seven of them look around at each other, waiting for someone to break the silence. They're supposedly seven Extra-Ordinary sixth-graders. Surely someone has some ideas?

Well. One of them does. It's Julie. Julie has some ideas.

She feels exhilarated. And terrified. But mostly exhilarated. She's pretty sure she just controlled a bunch of fish with her mind. And none of these people even seemed that freaked out about it.

Julie's willing to admit it: She can be a little intense. Most people don't like it. Or at least, the people at her middle school don't like it.

But this group, they seem different. They're all intense,

too, just like her. Li'l Kimmy's so chatty and is constantly bouncing around. Edwin spits out obscure facts like he's read every book in the world! And Dilip seems like this cool surfer kid—the kind of kid that would normally call her a freak—but he's also into Greek mythology! None of them seem quite like the kids at school who make fun of her.

Well, Maureen does. Seem that way. Maybe. Julie is still not totally sure about Maureen. Or Anton and Ting-Ting. But they seem more interested in what's going on now that they have nothing else to do.

So should she risk it? Should she come out of her shell? Onasander is either trying to kill them or challenge them. Either way, it's clear their lives depend on passing the tests.

"Okay, I have a confession," Julie says, tucking a flaming red lock behind her ear.

"What's up, Jules?" Li'l Kimmy says.

Julie's chest swells with warmth at the nickname. The first time Li'l Kimmy called her that, it seemed like a fluke, but the second time feels deliberate. Does that mean they're friends? Is this what friends do? Call each other nicknames and solve problems together? Will they have sleepovers and film TikToks and learn funny dances? If she's lucky, YES!

"Well, I can sort of read one of these languages."

"You can?" says Dilip, eyes wide.

Julie nods. "I wanted to read Sappho's poetry in its original language—I know, I know, so nerdy—"

"Nerdy?" Edwin says, brow furrowed and eyes wide. "That's, like, the coolest thing I've ever heard."

Encouraged, Julie smiles. "Well, I've been teaching myself ancient Greek dialects so that I could read it. And I picked up a little bit of Latin on the way. I'm not totally fluent in either, but . . ."

"You are such a queen!" Li'l Kimmy says, smacking Julie lightly on the shoulder.

"Does that even help us?" Ting-Ting asks. "Is this ancient Greek?"

"I believe so, yeah. And I think this one is Latin," Julie says.

"It sure is," says Edwin. "I can read Latin."

Julie grins. "Then between the two of us, we should be able to figure out what it says."

"Go ahead, geniuses," Maureen says, in an only slightly mocking tone. Edwin thinks that she's probably just jealous that she's not the one with the epic language skills.

"But what's the third language?" Li'l Kimmy asks.

"I don't know," Julie says, leaning closer. "These characters are completely unfamiliar. It almost looks . . . like an alien language or something. What do you think?" She looks over her shoulder at Edwin.

"No clue. I've never seen it before either."

"Well. Two out of three is not bad," says Julie. "If they all say the same thing, we only really need to translate one of them."

But before they can start, a voice comes from behind them.

From the river.

A voice like crystal and candy and clouds.

Chapter Seventeen

THE FIRE INSIDE

"Where's that coming from?" Li'l Kimmy asks.

The seven of them turn around. Edwin tenses up immediately. He wouldn't be surprised if a monster appeared at this point.

But it's not a monster. It's a girl. A girl?

"Over there." Julie points to the river.

A girl hangs with her elbows over the edge of the riverbank. She has white, almost glittering hair. There's something peculiar about her. All seven of them can't stop staring, completely forgetting about the task at hand.

The girl waves, and Li'l Kimmy realizes that she's not exactly, well, human. There's something between her fingers, like webbing. Is she a mermaid? But behind her, Li'l Kimmy can see legs kicking up. So no, not a mermaid.

"Who is she?" Dilip whispers, intrigued and a little afraid.

"I'm not sure, but I don't trust her," Julie says, crossing her arms.

"Hey over there!" the girl calls. "What're you all looking so serious about?" She has a tinkling voice, like bells and seashells clinking together.

Dilip starts walking toward the water.

"Dilip, where are you going?!" Edwin whisper-yells.

"What if she's lost?" He shrugs.

"*We're* lost, Dilip! We're the ones who are lost!" Julie exclaims.

But Dilip doesn't pay her any mind and continues to make his way toward the girl.

"This is ridiculous. We have to work on the puzzle! We have to keep moving!" Julie says, turning back to the tree trunk with the inscriptions on it. Maureen follows her, looking ready to get out of here as fast as possible.

"I'm going to check this out," Anton says. "She looks like a character from one of my games."

Ting-Ting, Li'l Kimmy, and Edwin follow them.

Li'l Kimmy feels torn. For some reason, she feels a pull to go speak with this girl. But, wait, what are they doing here again? She feels sort of fuzzy. She turns to Edwin.

"What now?" she says, head full of fluff.

"Uh, right. What were we just doing? Oh yeah, the puzzle, right. Why do we need to do that again?" Edwin wonders.

"'Cause Onasander told us to. . . . Right? And so we can get started on the lectures?" Li'l Kimmy answers, though what she's saying doesn't even make sense to her.

She and Edwin stare at each other for a few moments, their brains like mush. Why does everything suddenly seem so silly and pointless? They could just hang out here for a while. It might even be fun to go for a swim.

"What's going on? Why are we forgetting things? Do you feel weird?" Edwin asks Li'l Kimmy.

"It must have something to do with that girl. Look, you go stay with Julie and Maureen and work on the translation. I'm going to go get those guys away from whatever creature that is in the water."

They nod, high-five—clumsily—then go in opposite directions. The farther Edwin gets from the water, the clearer he feels, and by the time he's back at the tree trunk, he feels like himself again.

Li'l Kimmy, though, is feeling foggier and foggier, and *foggier* is a funny word if you think it too many times, she notices.

"Li'l Kimmy! Good, you're here!" Dilip says. "This is Daphne. She was just telling us about how there's this whole world under the water that's so beautiful."

Li'l Kimmy is having a hard time keeping things straight. Even if this strange brain fog wasn't clouding her vision and her mental capacities, she'd still have a hard time processing what's going on. So, okay. Focus, Li'l Kimmy. She's by a river, she's with this guy Dilip, who's with Ting-Ting and Anton. Where are they, again? And who's that new girl? Daphne. Right. Okay.

"That's great, Dilip! Glad to meet you, Daphne." Li'l Kimmy nods at her. "But we really have to be going—we're sort of on a mission here."

"Oh, just come relax!" Daphne says. "Sit down, put your feet in the water. Really, it's so nice."

Li'l Kimmy narrows her eyes in suspicion. She's so foggy.

"So what are you, a water nymph or something?" she says. If only this morning she knew that in earnestness she'd be asking some girl if she's a water nymph. What world are they in?

"Close!" Daphne says dreamily, splashing around.

"That looks fun," Anton says. "I wish I knew how to swim."

"Oh! I could teach you!" Daphne squeals, clapping her hands and flipping around in the water. "It will be so fun. Then you could come see my underwater world."

"I want to see the underwater world," Ting-Ting says wistfully. Her eyes have a glassy look to them, like she can't focus her vision.

Li'l Kimmy doesn't like the look in Ting-Ting's eyes. She looks completely untethered from reality. This realization makes her focus and clears her head for a moment.

There's something very wrong here. Dilip and Ting-Ting and Anton—their eyes are far, far away.

"You can come too!" Daphne says, reaching toward them.

Ting-Ting reaches out toward Daphne's outstretched arm.

"Water nymph," Li'l Kimmy says under her breath. "Not a water nymph . . . but close . . ."

This all reminds her of something. A class she had one time . . . some words . . . What were they? Why does her memory feel so distant?

"Come into the water, Anton," Daphne says, smiling. "Come and I'll teach you all about the water. It will be so wonderful."

Li'l Kimmy sits down. She's starting to see this girl's appeal. She's so beautiful, with that great voice, and she does look like she's having an amazing time in the water. . . .

"Okay, sure," Anton says.

He puts his feet in the water, and Daphne lifts her hands to help him in. Dilip is right behind him, waiting his turn.

"Dilip, something's not right," Li'l Kimmy says.

"Huh?" Dilip says, barely breaking eye contact with Daphne. Li'l Kimmy feels a creeping sensation come over her; something in the back of her mind flares.

"'The sea is lonely, the sea is dreary,'" Li'l Kimmy says, backing away from the water's edge, grabbing Ting-Ting.

"'The sea is restless and uneasy,'" she continues. "'Thou seekest quiet, thou art weary / Wandering thou knowest not whither.'"

"What on earth are you saying?" Ting-Ting cries. "Are you speaking English?!"

Li'l Kimmy's chest starts thumping. "The Sirens," the poem she became obsessed with by James Russell Lowell. About sirens luring sailors into the water's depths . . . forever.

"'Come and rest thee! Oh come hither / Come to this peaceful home of ours,'" she goes on.

Daphne's eyes widen, a look of fear coming over her face.

"'To the shore / Follow! Oh, follow! To be at rest forevermore! Forevermore!'" Li'l Kimmy gasps. She remembers the poem word for word. She thought it was incredible. Like a nineteenth-century rap. After she recites the poem, her mind feels crystal clear. On the shoreline, something flickers silver.

She bends over, heart pounding in her chest. She knows what it is. It's a puzzle piece. She looks up, expecting to see Dilip and Anton there to congratulate her, because they must be finished with this part of the test. But no, their minds still seem to be under the siren's control. And the puzzle piece is a lot smaller than the other ones. It almost looks as if it's half of one.

She grabs Dilip, whose arm is outstretched toward Daphne and the murky waters below.

"Dilip," Li'l Kimmy says, clutching his arm with one hand and her half puzzle piece with the other. "You said you like mythology. Well, what do you know about sirens?"

This question seems to bring Dilip back to reality, if only slightly. His eyes start to clear; his brow furrows.

"Sirens lure mortals to the water," he says, looking confused. "They make you want to follow them. . . ."

His eyes grow wide.

"And then they drown you! You walk right into your own death!" Li'l Kimmy finishes.

"Oh, this is bad. This is very bad," Dilip says. He looks around. "Wait. Where are Anton and Ting-Ting?"

Li'l Kimmy shakes her head, clearing away the last of the fog. She spots them. They're both in the water up to their knees. Daphne is holding each of their hands in her webbed fingers.

"We have to do something, QUICK," Dilip says. "But we can't get in the water, or we might *all* get pulled under." He presses his hands to his temples. "Ugh! She's still trying to get into my head!"

Li'l Kimmy feels anger building and building in her. She hasn't let herself feel like this for such a long time. She can't even remember the last time she let any anger show. Because if you're angry, it means you care. If you're upset, it means you're invested in something. And you might be made fun of for that. You might be told you're being "crazy" or being "too much." But right now? *This* is what's crazy. A siren is about to drown two of her teammates! Or whatever they are. She has to do something. If there's one thing Li'l Kimmy hates, it's when people lie. She can't stand poseurs. And Daphne is the biggest poseur of them all.

A weird feeling starts in Li'l Kimmy's chest. Hot, lava-like. Does she have heartburn?

"Anton, Ting-Ting, you've got to get out of the water! NOW!" Dilip shouts.

"But it's sooo peaceful," Ting-Ting says, floating on her back.

Anton starts slipping under the water a little. He still can't swim. But he's so lost in Daphne's spell, he doesn't seem to notice.

"Let me help you, Anton," Daphne says. "I'll teach you to swim. You'll never want to leave! You can swim with me forever."

"What are you guys doing over there?!" Maureen shouts. "We need your help!"

"We're having a little bit of a crisis here, Maureen!" Dilip shouts back. "Anton and Ting-Ting are being mind-controlled to their deaths by a siren!"

"Ugh! Just leave them!" Maureen yells.

What? thinks Dilip.

He looks at Li'l Kimmy and blanches slightly. "Li'l Kimmy, are you . . . okay?"

Li'l Kimmy is not okay. Li'l Kimmy is pissed off. And her whole body feels like it's burning. Burning with the anger. Burning at the injustice. Burning with years of pent-up emotion.

Daphne grabs Anton's hands and starts pulling him slowly toward her. His mouth fills with water. He coughs, throwing his head up for air, but it barely clears the surface.

Li'l Kimmy walks to the very edge of the river, ignoring Dilip, watching Daphne. The hot, molten feeling keeps rising. Daphne is this beautiful siren just acting like everything is fine, but in truth she's about to drown them! The feeling of being lied to, being manipulated, is making her eyes hot. She feels like she could burst into tears—no, that's not it. Not tears. Something else.

"Say goodbye," Daphne coos, and begins to pull both Ting-Ting and Anton underneath the waves.

"No!" Dilip cries.

Then . . .

Release!

A sizzle. A scream. The scent of burning hair and burnt seaweed in the air.

"What was that?!" Daphne screams, relinquishing her hold on Anton and Ting-Ting.

"Li'l Kimmy!" exclaims Dilip. "What are you—"

A fireball shoots across the water, singeing Daphne's arm. She shrieks in anger, and suddenly they all notice that her teeth are pointed. And since when were her eyes completely black?

Dilip dives in and grabs Anton, pulling him to the shore. Ting-Ting comes to her senses and follows. Anton coughs up river water, but he's all right. Ting-Ting looks confused.

"You guys okay?" Dilip asks.

Anton's about to answer, but Li'l Kimmy interrupts.

"You guys? RUN!"

Dilip looks up at the water. Daphne is slowly moving toward them, and she looks . . . murderous.

Anton and Ting-Ting scramble to their feet, and the four of them tear back through the underbrush to the tree where the others are waiting.

"What happened?" Edwin asks. "What's going on? And why are you soaking wet all over again?"

"We need to get out of here," Dilip says, pointing back toward the river. "Now!"

Daphne's beautiful white hair is now scraggly, filled with dirt and pebbles from the river. Her skin is a pale green, and her mossy dress is sopping and brown at the edges. And those eyes. Those black eyes. She walks toward them like a zombie on the hunt, her sharp teeth and sharp fingernails itching to get into their flesh.

"Wow. She could use a makeover," says Maureen.

"Stay away!" Li'l Kimmy screams, the feeling welling up in her again. Then a sphere of pure fire shoots out and lands in Daphne's chest, pushing her back into the water with a harsh sizzling sound. A bloodcurdling scream rips through the hot, humid air.

Li'l Kimmy feels faint. She swerves, losing her footing. Dilip catches her before she hits the ground.

The group stares at her in disbelief. When she opens her eyes, she sees them all standing over her. "What?"

"You just . . ." Dilip starts.

"I'm pretty sure that you . . ." Edwin points toward the fire and smoke rising off the river.

"That was *sick!*" Anton exclaims.

"No, no, no!" Ting-Ting squeals, clearly terrified.

"Li'l Kimmy, I think we need to talk," Julie says.

Li'l Kimmy just wobbles in Dilip's grip. Then she stands up and rubs her eyes. Why do they feel so hot? "What are you guys freaking out about?"

"The fire," Edwin says.

"Yeah, where did that come from?"

"Li'l Kimmy," Julie says, putting her hands on Li'l Kimmy's shoulders. "It came from you."

Chapter Eighteen

RING OF FIRE

"**M**e?" Li'l Kimmy asks. She feels like she's going to faint all over again.

"I gotcha," Dilip says, holding her up.

"What—how? And why? And how? And when and how? AND HOW?!" She feels dizzy. She feels nauseated. She feels . . . elated? "What do you mean it came from me?" she asks. "How?"

"FROM YOUR EYES!" they all say in unison.

For once, something all of them can agree on.

"Does being in this place give us, like, powers?" Ting-Ting asks. "Like, is that part of the Octagon Valley Institute somehow? Is it a new technology?"

The seven of them look at each other, tingles all around.

"I guess that's possible," Edwin says, scratching his

head. "Though I'm not sure exactly how just being in a place would give us powers. Or why."

"Is any of this real? I'm so confuuuused," Ting-Ting whines.

"Yeah, so where are my powers?" Anton says. He squints his eyes at the river.

"What are you trying to do?" Maureen scoffs.

"I'm trying to shoot fire out of my eyes! If she can do it, why can't I?" Anton replies.

But no fire emerges from his eyes. Nice try, Anton. Maybe in your next life.

"Guess you just don't have the touch." Maureen shrugs smugly.

"I don't understand how this is possible," Li'l Kimmy says. "Powers? Like, for real?"

Edwin is about to say something but thinks better of it. What are you hiding, Edwin?

"Hey, by the way," Anton says, turning around. "Thanks for telling Dilip and Li'l Kimmy to leave us back there, Maureen."

"Yeah, what was that about? We would've been trapped in the underwater city forever!" Ting-Ting cries.

"I hate to break it to you, Ting-Ting," Dilip says, "but I don't think there's an underwater city. The underwater city is . . . uh . . . well, the afterlife."

Ting-Ting's eyes go wide as moons. "No . . ."

"Yeah. The Big D," Dilip says, nodding.

"So you really think Octagon would have let us . . . Big D?" Ting-Ting says.

"I kind of think maybe he would have," Dilip says, swallowing hard.

While Ting-Ting processes this information, Li'l Kimmy notices something sparkling in the sun near her feet. Yup, there it is. The other half of her puzzle piece. She grabs it and stands up. "We got another!" She tosses both pieces to Dilip.

"Nice," he says, though there isn't much enthusiasm behind it this time.

Thinking about the Big D will do that to a person.

Julie, who's been working at the tree trunk again, turns around excitedly. "I think I've got it!"

"Great, because I'd love to level out of here already," says Anton.

The group crowds around her.

"*In girum imus nocte et consumimur igni,*'" Julie says, pointing to the tree trunk. "'We enter the circle after dark and are consumed by fire.' Right, Edwin?"

Edwin nods.

"Whoa," Dilip says. "That sounds, uh, rather unpleasant."

"So . . . what now? We just say it out loud and the door opens?" Anton asks.

"She just said it out loud, moron," says Maureen.

"Try again," Edwin suggests.

Julie moves to stand directly in front of the tree trunk.

She says it again, this time slowly, with force. *"In circum post tenebras imus et igni consumimur."*

They all hold their breath. Julie's not sure how good her Latin pronunciation is. Is her interpretation correct?

She tries it one more time. But louder. Possibly louder than she's ever said anything. It feels kinda good.

"In circum post tenebras imus et igni consumimur!"

The door in the tree trunk opens. Through the doorframe is a dark room filled with a circle of fire.

"Are you sure that's right?" Ting-Ting says. "That doesn't look right."

"I really think that was right." Julie frowns. "But I'll try again." She closes the door, and she and Edwin confer once more. She alters the pronunciation slightly, rounding her *o*'s.

But this time, after she says the words and the door opens once more, they see an empty room with a nuclear warhead exploding inside.

"SHUT IT!" Edwin yells, shoving the door closed.

"I don't know about you guys, but I definitely prefer the first option," Dilip says. "Less immediately lethal."

"I think your pronunciation was right the first time," Edwin says.

"So, we have to go into the fire room?" says Ting-Ting timidly.

Edwin nods. "I think that every time we solve a piece of the puzzle, it's just going to take us somewhere more and more dangerous."

"The fire looked pretty scary," Anton says.

"Yeah. Unfortunately, I think we're on the right track," Edwin tells them.

Julie takes a big breath. "So," she says, "out of the frying pan and into the fire?"

Chapter Nineteen

SQUARE BREATHING IN A CIRCLE

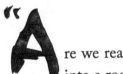re we really going to do this?" Anton asks. "Walk into a room filled with fire?"

"It's kind of hot," Ting-Ting adds.

"Better than the nuclear-bomb room, at least," Dilip ventures.

"I don't think we have a choice," Julie says. "We have to keep moving forward."

They step inside, and the door shuts behind them. The room, if it is a room, is completely dark, lit only by the flames licking the air in a ring.

The only thing they can see, besides the fire, is something glinting on the ground. Li'l Kimmy approaches it, cautiously. Sure enough, it's the next puzzle piece. Silver, light, with the line going through it in another strange shape.

"You still got room in those pockets of yours, Dilip?" she asks.

He pats his board shorts, looking fearful for a moment. What if he lost one when he jumped in the water to save Anton for the second time? But yes, thankfully, they're all still there, along with the Hot Cheetos. These board shorts are serious business, made for keeping things safe when skating or surfing. Or, he supposes, going on some bizarre and life-threatening adventure. He adds this fifth puzzle piece to his pocket.

"What now?" Ting-Ting says, staring fearfully at the flames. They are at least ten feet tall.

Julie thinks back to the inscription. "The message said 'We enter the circle after dark and are consumed by fire.' That sort of reads as instructions, right?"

"But do we really have to be consumed by fire?" Maureen questions.

"*Consumed* doesn't necessarily mean we die, right?" Edwin says. "*Consume* can have various meanings. Metaphorical meanings, too."

Ah, finally some metaphor! Things have been getting a bit literal at Octagon Valley. . . .

"Maybe it's not a real fire?" Li'l Kimmy posits. She walks up to it and puts her hands close to the flame. She almost swipes her whole hand through it, but Edwin grabs her elbow at the last second.

"Li'l Kimmy!" he says. "What are you doing?!"

"I was just gonna test it." She shrugs.

"With your own hand?!"

On second thought, that impulse doesn't seem so good.

"Maybe the fire consumes us to take us to the next place," Dilip tries out.

"Or maybe it burns us to death," Ting-Ting says.

"Things have been so strange in this place," Julie says, "I wouldn't be that surprised if this fire didn't even burn."

"Not like the fire that comes out of Li'l Kimmy's eyes!" Dilip cracks a grin. "That definitely burns."

He holds his hand up for a high five, which Li'l Kimmy accepts with a bashful smile. She's still unclear if this new development is something to be smiling about.

"You know what?" Dilip says, nodding. "I'll go first. I've always wanted to do that thing where you walk across coals really fast without burning your feet. Maybe this will be like an extreme version of that."

"Are we even sure that we're supposed to go into the ring of fire?" Ting-Ting asks.

"I don't think we're sure about anything in this place, but what choice do we have? The door closed behind us," Julie says.

"So let's just open it again." Ting-Ting goes to where she

thinks the door is and finds nothing. Just a smooth wall that feels like rock. The door has disappeared like all the others.

"Okay, so we're trapped," she says. "Unless anyone's new superpower is magically making doors appear?"

Silence, except for the roaring of the flames.

"We need to move forward," Edwin says.

"I think Edwin's right," Julie agrees. "This is definitely another of Onasander's obstacles. Why else would the puzzle piece appear?"

"All right, I'm going for it," Dilip decides.

"Dilip, are you sure?" Julie says.

He nods to the six of them and takes a deep breath. The ring of fire with walls of flames ten feet high flickers and thrashes in front of him in the pitch black. Dilip has always sought out an adrenaline rush. What's skateboarding and surfing if not an adrenaline rush? This is just like that. Except there's the very real possibility that he could burn alive.

He takes a step forward, feeling the adrenaline pumping through his body. There's no burning sensation on his skin, just a light heat. And then, after he enters the ring, the ground seems to fall out from under his feet. He drops, drops, drops, for so long that he almost stops feeling the sensation of dropping, and it just feels like he's floating. Then his descent gets progressively slower, as if some strange accident of gravity allows him to lower gently to the ground.

Dilip laughs. That was actually kind of fun. "Hey!" he shouts, tilting his head back. "If you can hear me up there, I'm fine! Come join me!"

But he gets no answer in return.

Back in the hall of flames, Li'l Kimmy, Edwin, Julie, Maureen, Anton, and Ting-Ting stand quietly, trying to assess what has happened to Dilip.

"I didn't hear any screaming," Ting-Ting whispers, her eyes welling with tears.

"Or yelling out for us, or warning," Julie adds.

"Do you think it worked?" Edwin asks.

"Either it worked or something very bad happened," Maureen replies.

They all look around at each other fearfully. Julie is impressed that Dilip went through the fire so easily, and alone. She feels a sudden itch at the back of her throat. What's that feeling? Oh no. Oh *no*. It's tears. She doesn't want to cry in front of these people! She really doesn't. But suddenly, she's feeling incredibly overwhelmed.

What is this place? Where are they? The concept of death is so abstract it usually feels almost meaningless. But now, facing flames, adrenaline still coursing through her from being in the river, somehow controlling the minds of animals, and cracking an ancient code, it feels more real.

She's never felt so alive before, or so terrified. And who are these people she's with? Are they her friends, or are they just a random collection of strangers? Do they even care about her? Does she care about them? Why can't they just break out of this place?! She wishes she could teleport far, far away from here. To her orchestra. To her bedroom. Maybe even to her middle school. There she'd be taunted or ignored, but at least she wouldn't be fighting for her life. Whoever this Onasander Octagon is, he's evil.

Edwin sees Julie breathing at an increasingly intense rate. Her chest is rising and falling so quickly that he can tell what's coming. Panic attack. He knows the signs well.

"Julie, what's wrong with you?" Maureen snickers.

Julie quickly wipes a tear from her eye.

Ting-Ting, as if panic attacks are contagious, bursts into soft sobbing. Like she's finally been given permission to emote.

"Oh, come on now, we're devolving into chaos!" Maureen cries.

Edwin walks over to Julie and puts his hands on her shoulders. "Hey, it's okay. I know how you're feeling."

"Wh-what?" she says between choppy breaths.

"I have a trick for it. Just breathe in for four seconds, hold for four seconds, breath out for four, hold for four. And repeat it." He looks over his shoulder to where Ting-Ting is crying in the corner. "Ting-Ting, you too," he says.

Ting-Ting only sobs louder. But Julie does as she's told, and she can feel her nervous system begin to calm. Li'l Kimmy can tell that she's still holding a lot of emotion in. Her whole body is tense. Li'l Kimmy knows that feeling too.

"Julie, you can let yourself cry," she says softly, thinking of how she felt by the river when she finally let out her anger. "It's a good release. It's okay. It'll make you feel better."

"I don't have to cry," Julie gulps out. "I'm fine."

Edwin and Li'l Kimmy look at each other skeptically.

"I think you do, and that's okay," Li'l Kimmy says.

Julie has never had anyone her age be so gentle with her. They're being so nice that it makes her eyes well even worse. Finally, she lets go. Rivers of tears cover her cheeks. "I just—I don't—I don't know why this is happening to us," she says.

"Onasander," Anton says, biting his nails nervously. "He's like the final boss."

"Ugh, you guys!" Maureen interrupts. "Yeah, maybe Onasander is an evil freak, but we have to suck it up and keep moving. Look, Julie and Ting-Ting, you obviously can't handle this, so maybe you should just stay here and the rest of us will keep going."

"Stay here?" Ting-Ting exclaims. "Stay in this room of fire?! How do we know what happens if we stay behind?!"

"We don't." Maureen shrugs.

"Jeez, do you have a heart?" Edwin asks her. "No way. They're not staying behind."

"Fine. Well, then let's get a move on." Maureen rolls her eyes.

"Why are you not freaked out by all this, Maureen?" Li'l Kimmy says, hands on her hips. "The rest of us have had breakdowns at some point or another, and this whole time you've just been acting like all this is normal."

"And trying to leave people behind," Anton adds.

Maureen pauses, looking stupefied. Then she recovers her judgmental resting face.

"Guess I'm just better equipped for all this than you are. Not my problem. I'm a New Yorker, after all."

"Yeah, a New Yorker who spends all her time in her daddys' penthouse, or being chaperoned around the city in a black SUV. I doubt New York has hardened you," Li'l Kimmy spits out.

She doesn't mean to be mean, but Maureen's really getting on her nerves with her attitude.

"Whatever." Maureen rolls her eyes.

"Nice comeback, genius," Li'l Kimmy says.

"Okay, okay, you two," Julie interjects, wiping her eyes. "Truce. We do need to keep moving. We can't leave Dilip alone, wherever he is."

"Fine," Li'l Kimmy says, holding her hand out for a handshake with Maureen. "Truce."

Maureen just slaps the hand away and crosses her arms.

"Wow! So mature!" Li'l Kimmy snaps.

"Hey," Anton says, piping up for the first time in forever. "You guys don't have to like each other, but you have to work together, all right? We have a common goal, if nothing else."

Everyone looks to Anton, shocked.

"What? That's just common sense for a quest adventure. Happens all the time in games. You don't have to like your comrades, you just have to work with them."

"He's right," Edwin says. "It's time we cross over. You all ready?"

The six of them look skeptically at one another. Tear-streaked faces, angry glances, deep breaths. There's only one way out of this hot, stuffy, freaky room. Through the fire.

Chapter Twenty

LEVELING UP

"**F**inally!" Dilip says. "What took you so long?"

He flips the sixth silver puzzle piece in the air, tossing it and catching it as he watches each of the six of them land softly. He's looking a little show-offy, but that's part of the charm of Dilip, isn't it?

"Where are we?" Julie asks, looking around.

They've walked through flames, fallen through some other kind of void, only to emerge in a . . . medieval castle? They're in the middle of a stone bridge between two towers. From their vantage, they can see faraway fields and distant villages.

"No idea," says Dilip. "Scotland?"

"At least it seems safe so far," Li'l Kimmy says. "Have you come across anyone? Or anything?"

"Nope, just me," Dilip says.

Julie turns around and shades her eyes against the sun. It appears he spoke too soon.

"You guys, I think we have company," Julie says.

"Cool!" Anton yells, enthusiastic for once. "Assassins!"

Only Anton would cheer at the sight of murderers-for-hire.

Li'l Kimmy has never thought about what an assassin might look like, but apparently they wear matching black outfits, black hoods over their heads, and black scarves that cover their faces. It seems that Anton is more than familiar with assassin garb from all his time gaming. To him, it looks like seven celebrities are rushing the castle.

"I wouldn't exactly say this is cool, Anton," Maureen says, moving into the nearest tower and looking out the window. "They're on their way up."

Sure enough, the assassins have started scaling the tower below Maureen's window. With their bare hands. No picks, no axes, no cords or carabiners. It's actually totally creepy.

"Any chance your video games taught you what to do to stave off assassins?" Edwin asks, running his hand over his hair. He sees blades on the hips of the assassins, and they look sharp.

"The main difference between an assassin and a regular killer," Anton says, eyes fixed on the climbers, "is that assassins are extensively battle-trained, whereas most regular killers have no skills whatsoever."

"Great," Dilip says, pacing, "that's just great. So not only do they have weapons, they're really good at using them."

"Guys! Over here!" They all turn to see Julie beckoning them from the other tower. "I think there might be a way out."

"Worth a try," Dilip says. "Let's go."

Maureen joins them as they jog over to join Julie, but Anton lingers in the center of the bridge.

"Anton," Li'l Kimmy shouts, turning around. "What are you doing? Come on!"

Anton looks down at the quickly ascending assassins.

"I think I'm gonna stay."

"WHAT?!" the six others shriek.

"I want to see what my powers are!" he says, as if it were the most obvious thing in the world.

"We don't even know if these powers are real," Julie says. "It could just be an illusion of Octagon Valley! Like some sort of new tech!"

"Even so, I still want to see what mine are. And I think they'll come out if I fight these assassins."

"Anton, come on, we can test it some other time, like when we get out of this place!" Dilip yells.

"I've always wanted to fight assassins. You guys all got to do your own stuff, now I want to try!" Anton says.

"Guys, we don't have that much time until the assassins get here. Just let him do what he wants!" Maureen chimes in.

"There you go, wanting to leave people behind again!"

Julie pipes up. "He's going to get totally chopped to bits by those guys. Have you seen their knives? They probably have throwing stars too!"

"Ooh! I hope so!" Anton claps.

"We can't force him to do something he doesn't want to do," Maureen argues. "And he wants to test his skills! I think that's brave."

Anton smiles proudly.

"Anton, this isn't a video game," Edwin warns, walking toward him. "This is real life."

"You think I don't know that?" Anton snaps. "Do you think I'm stupid? I know the difference. I'm smart too, you know. I came here because Octagon has the most advanced tech in the world, and I wanted in on that. I just don't spend all my time being a dork, like you. I have millions of followers who watch me play."

Edwin, hurt, puts his hands up in surrender and walks away. "Fine. Your choice, I guess," he says. "I can't stop you."

"This really doesn't seem like a good idea, Anton," Li'l Kimmy says in a last-ditch effort. "The assassins are right there!"

"And I'm ready for them! Don't worry, guys. You go ahead, I'll take care of them! This is where I belong!"

Dilip, Julie, Edwin, and Li'l Kimmy look at each other. Are they seriously just going to let Anton get slashed by assassins? But barring physical force, how can they convince him otherwise?

The seven assassins crawl over the edge of the window and lower themselves into the tower and onto the bridge, circling Anton with their knives drawn. Edwin can just barely see their eyes between the cloth of their scarves.

"I've totally got this covered, guys," Anton says, arms outstretched.

The assassins lunge toward him and Anton lets out a—quite impressive, actually—battle cry. But rather than attack Anton, the assassins lift him up above their heads. They start walking in the opposite direction of the rest of the group, Anton raised high.

"Wait!" Anton says to them. "What are you doing?! I have to show you my sick moves!"

As they breach the doorway into the tower, as if entering a portal, the assassins and Anton all disappear. The last thing they hear is Anton yelling, "Don't worry about me, guys! I'm sure my powers will kick in any minute now!"

Chapter Twenty-One

THE META MAZE

Bye, Anton! He wasn't so bad, but we won't miss him either, will we?

Still, the group is silent as they walk in the opposite direction from where Anton was taken. When they pass through the doorway to the second tower, they find themselves standing in front of a courtyard surrounded by a massive set of hedges with an opening in the middle.

Dilip feels a swelling of awe. If this whole experience, all of the Octagon Valley Institute, is an extended maze, then now he's in a maze within a maze. How meta.

"That was so messed up," Edwin says in a quiet voice. "I can't believe we just let him get carried off."

"They're not going to hurt him." Maureen shrugs.

"How do you know that?" Edwin snaps. "How could

you possibly know that? First we leave Harold behind, now Anton? What are we doing?"

"We're doing the best we can, Edwin," Ting-Ting says softly. "Let's just focus on where we are now and what we can control." It's something her mother always says.

Edwin crosses his arms over his chest.

"Yeah, I don't like it either," Li'l Kimmy says. "I mean, what if this is just a whole big plan to try and get rid of us? Pick us off, one by one. I mean, isn't that what villains do?"

"But why would Onasander Octagon want to get rid of us?" Edwin asks.

"Beats me. But I mean . . ." Li'l Kimmy wonders if she should tell them what she's been thinking. "Look, we all passed some crazy assessment, right? Like, we're the smartest people in our generation, right?"

She feels a little braggy just saying it. But hey, just stating the obvious here.

"Right," says Julie. "What are you getting at?"

"And what do supervillains do?" Li'l Kimmy says. "They get rid of their nemeses."

"Uh . . . how are we his nemeses?" Julie asks.

"We're not *yet*. But we're all *Extra-Ordinary*, right? He determined it with his assessment. So what if he's trying to get rid of us now? While we're still young. Before we can grow up to threaten his chokehold of influence and power, and before we're old enough to challenge him or, you know, drive."

Edwin laughs. "Li'l Kimmy, I think you've watched too many movies."

"Okay, okay, fine. It was just a theory. So, what now?" she asks. "We enter the maze?"

"Looks like it," Edwin says, nodding.

The six of them walk toward the opening between the hedges, ready to cross into whatever awaits them inside. But when they get there, they find they can't cross into the maze at all. It feels as if there's a slightly bouncy glass door keeping them out.

"An invisible shield?" Edwin asks.

"This place just gets weirder and weirder." Li'l Kimmy shakes her head.

"Maybe we can't all go at once," Dilip says. "Like, maybe we have to go one at a time."

"Great, splitting up so each of us can get carried off by assassins," Edwin says under his breath.

"I can't go by myself!" Ting-Ting cries. "I need someone to tell me what to do!"

"I can go first again," Dilip says. He's still riding the high of walking through the fire unscathed. He feels pretty much invincible right now. He shoves losing Anton out of his mind. He doesn't really care about Harold. That guy seemed like a waste of space.

Harsh, Dilip! But Harold will be fine. Maybe one day he'll break from the line of Harolds and form his own identity. Stranger things have happened, right? Like, well, all of this.

"How do we know when we'll meet up again? What if we get lost?" Julie asks.

"Good point." Edwin considers. "Maybe we can have a code word we yell out if we're trying to meet up with each other?"

"How about *Daedalus*?" Dilip asks, excitedly. "*Looking for Daedalus*? And we respond *Theseus is here* if we hear the call. And if we sense any danger, we say *The Minotaur is coming*? You know, from Daedalus's labyrinth. From the Greek myth? The Minotaur is the terrifying thing in the middle, and Theseus kills the Minotaur."

Julie smiles. This plan is so Dilip, and she likes that she knows someone well enough to think that a plan is so them.

"I like it," Edwin says. "It fits."

"I just hope there aren't any actual Minotaurs," Ting-Ting says nervously.

"Well, if there are, we'll figure out how to beat them," Dilip says with a confident grin.

But the grin doesn't work on Ting-Ting. She backs up a step. She's actually wringing her hands. "I'm not going."

Li'l Kimmy rolls her eyes, feeling like Maureen. "What do you mean you're not going?"

"I'm done with this," says Ting-Ting.

"I hear you," says Maureen. "What's Onasander's deal?

Why are we here? Why are we doing this? I doubt there's even a way to win it. We don't even know how to enter this stupid maze."

After Li'l Kimmy posited that Onasander is trying to get rid of them while they are still young, they aren't as shocked at Maureen's harsh words, and Edwin considers them thoughtfully. He's always one to look at all sides of the story.

"You're right, Maureen," Edwin says. "There is no way to win it. And I think that's the point. I believe that we're in a maze of parallel worlds—alternate realities. A maze-like replica of the multiverse, if you will. Which means that everything is possible, and everything is random. There are no patterns when everything is an option."

"But that's so annoying!" Li'l Kimmy says, tossing her head back.

"I agree," Edwin says. "All of us are the kinds of kids who want an answer for everything. We want to *know*. We want to be able to decipher the world, figure things out, break down the pieces and understand them. But some-times, things are just random! Sometimes you just have to roll the dice." A motto for gamblers everywhere. Wonder if Edwin's ever been to Vegas.

Julie nods.

"The longer we take trying to figure things out, the lon-ger it will take for us to get out of this maze. Sometimes,

I guess, you just have to move through the randomness, quickly and confidently," Edwin continues.

"In a way," Li'l Kimmy notes, "that's sort of a pattern within itself. The pattern of no pattern."

"A nice way to think of it." Edwin smiles. "Now, I guess we just have to keep moving through as quickly as we can until we get to the end. What do you say, everyone?"

"Let's do it!" Dilip pumps his fist in the air.

"I told you, I'm not going." It's Ting-Ting. She's sitting now, her back against the hedge. She has an intense expression of certainty on her face. It's the first time Julie can remember her looking resolute.

"What do you *mean* you're not going?" Edwin asks.

"I'm tired of this. Of all this. I don't want to do it anymore. This whole thing is nothing like what I thought it was going to be."

"Yeah, clearly!" Dilip says. Julie shoots him a look, and he softens. "I just mean none of us thought it would turn out like this. We all thought we were going to a three-day academic conference, right?"

They all nod.

"But we don't really have a choice. What are you going to do, just stay here forever?"

"I might!" Ting-Ting says. "I lost my notebook! Do you even know what that means for me?!"

They all stare at her. Who even uses notebooks anymore?

"It means that for the first time maybe ever, I feel free. I don't have to write everything down. I don't have to worry about what I might be missing. I don't have to think about what my mom might ask me later and whether I have all the details she wants to hear. I don't have to take notes for any more tests—I mean assessments! I'm free!"

"Whoa," says Dilip. "That notebook was more than just a notebook."

"Plus, staying put is much better than wandering around in horribly dangerous multiverses forever," Ting-Ting says with a nod. "So I'm staying."

"But what will happen to you, Ting-Ting?" Li'l Kimmy says.

"I don't care! I'm done."

"Maybe we should just let her stay," Maureen says.

Edwin turns to her angrily. "Why are you so intent on letting everyone stay behind?!"

"Why are you so intent on forcing everyone to come with you?" Maureen snaps back. "Is it because you never had friends before?"

Edwin recoils, a spike of hurt cutting through his heart.

"Whoa, whoa, whoa, that was way harsh, Maureen," Li'l Kimmy says. "Why do you have to be so mean?"

"Mean? I'm just being realistic. We need to get a move on. If Ting-Ting doesn't want to come, why should we force her?"

"She's right. You're better off without me. I'm just not like the rest of you," Ting-Ting says, head in her hands.

"What do you mean like the rest of us?" Dilip asks.

"You guys are special. You even have special powers," Ting-Ting says.

"Well, not all of us." Dilip shrugs. So far, all he's useful for is collecting puzzle pieces in his cargo shorts. But he's okay with that. Sort of. And Maureen's got nothing, unless her superpower is being a jerk.

Ting-Ting ignores him. "Edwin can move things with his mind, Julie can control minds with her music, and Li'l Kimmy can shoot fire from her eyes. I'm sure you and Maureen will prove yourselves sooner or later." She appeals to them. "You're all special, and you know it. I'm not special. And for the first time, I think that's okay. The thing is, I didn't even see the one hundred and eighth question."

"The what?" asks Dilip.

"The question, remember? On the OVAEO? The only one that mattered," she explains. "My mom . . . my mom kept bugging my teacher. To find out how they graded the Octagon Valley Assessment. Wanted to find out why I didn't pass. My mom wouldn't give up, so my teacher gave in. She told my mom the only question that mattered was seeing the one hundred and eighth one, and that the answer was *yes*."

Edwin furrowed his brow. He remembered the 108th

question. It read: *Do you see this question?* He had answered *Yes.* He thought it might have been a trick of some sort.

"The thing is, not everyone could see the question, so if you saw it, you were special," Ting-Ting explains. "But I never saw it. I cheated. Like Harold."

(Remember Harold?)

The five of them pause, taking this in. Edwin's always known he is special. But Julie squirms, feeling guilty for seeing the question. Li'l Kimmy shrugs. She saw the question—so what? Dilip can't even remember if he saw the question, but he must have, since he's here.

"Look, whether you cheated or not, for the first time this entire time, you're making a decision for yourself," Maureen declares. She looks around at the group. "This whole day, she's just been doing whatever you guys tell her to. This is the first time she's standing up for herself. And you just want to shoot her down?"

Dilip considers this. "I guess that makes sense." He's never been great at conflict management. He usually just avoids it; he's good at skating over many kinds of surfaces.

"Are you seriously agreeing with her, Dilip?" Julie yelps. "You're going to just let Ting-Ting stay here?"

Dilio doesn't respond.

"Hey! Dilip! Earth to Dilip?!" Julie says, waving a hand in front of his face. "Can you just focus for one single second?"

"I don't know!" Dilip says, snapping back into it, feeling attacked. "I don't know what the right thing to do is."

"Great," Julie goes on. "So you'd just leave one of us behind to fend for ourselves. All of you would? You'd just leave any of us behind at any moment? I guess so, huh? We've left two behind already."

"Julie, I think you're overreacting a little bit. You're always so negative," Li'l Kimmy says.

"Really? Well, I'm sorry for actually *having* emotions and not just being the cool, chill girl who raps. Sorry that I am *honest* about how I'm feeling."

"Hey," Li'l Kimmy says softly, wounded.

"This is getting ugly really fast," Edwin says, pushing his glasses back up the bridge of his nose. "Why don't you two just apologize to each other, and we can move on."

"Us?" Li'l Kimmy says. "What about Dilip? Why is it only the girls who have to apologize to each other?"

"Yeah," Maureen chimes in. "And who put you in charge, anyway?"

Edwin feels everything unraveling. If they bonded quickly, it feels like they're un-bonding just as fast. He sort of did fancy himself the leader of the group, he realizes. Was that delusional or egotistical of him?

"Okay, whatever, you guys do whatever you want," Maureen says. "I'm going to go my own way. See you around. If only one of us can enter at a time, then here I go."

With that, Maureen enters the maze.

Huh. It works.

"Seriously? Wow. Okay, cool," Julie says. "I'm glad we all matter so much to each other."

"You know what? I think I'll try being on my own, too. It's getting way too stressful being around you guys," Li'l Kimmy says.

And with that, Li'l Kimmy disappears into the hedges.

"Well, this is just amazing," Julie says, hands on hips. "Edwin? What now?"

"Don't look at me!" he snaps. "You heard Maureen, I'm not in charge." He's always found it easier to be alone, anyway. Makes sense that nothing would change, even at Octagon Valley. Edwin practically throws himself into the maze.

"I'd say we should go together," Dilip adds with a yawn, "but I'd probably just be way too *distracted* to be a good teammate. Later, Julie."

Then Julie is the only one left.

Well, not the only one.

"Thanks a lot, Ting-Ting. I hope this is what you wanted." Then Julie storms into the maze too.

Ting-Ting, finally alone in the courtyard, closes her eyes and falls asleep.

Chapter Twenty-Two

GETTING BEAT

This was certainly not how Julie envisioned things going. Or maybe it was. Maybe it was predictable that things would fall apart. Had she been kidding herself by thinking that she'd emerge from this weekend with friends? That now seems as likely as listening to Onasander's lecture series before the three days are over.

She's not sure where she is, exactly, or what the plan is. Are they all just going to wander around this maze forever? Will they ever find the exit? And what's this weird room she's in, anyway? It has an almost familiar smell to it. Like bologna and chocolate milk. Like plastic and sweat. Like . . . oh no.

"Julie, is that you?"

Julie turns around, and there she is. It's like a time

warp, except she's only time-warped back a few days. To Connecticut. To her middle school. To real life. Was all of this a dream? Is she just back where she's always been, sitting alone in the cafeteria?

"Gosh, Julie, always such a loner."

It's Clarissa and Lauren, standing by their cafeteria table where a dozen friends are all swapping phones back and forth, showing each other videos, memes, songs. Stealing each other's hats, trading lunches. And Julie is standing right by the table she always sits at alone, in the corner, with her large book of Sappho's poetry or whatever fantasy book she's reading that week. The books are like her protection. And it usually works well. No one bothers her at lunch anymore. Well, no one except for Clarissa and Lauren, who seem to always have it out for her. She barely makes it through a week without some snide comment from them about something she's wearing or the fact that she's always alone.

The worst part is, she can't tell what stings more: having those snide comments hurled at her or being totally ignored. At least when they make fun of her, she knows she exists. Still, it hurts. Boy, does it hurt.

The Octagon Valley Institute was supposed to be a fresh start. Her besties—otherwise known as her parents—were getting worried about her. Only ever hanging out with grown-ups who play musical instruments is not exactly normal for a girl her age. Especially since she is sort of their boss. But alas, this weekend has not turned out to be a fresh start. In fact, it hurts worse than ever, because she thought she was really on the way to making friends. Clearly that was just an illusion.

Like everything else in this place.

Like everything else in this place.

Hold on. She's not really in her cafeteria, is she? She's in Octagon's maze. Which means this isn't her reality. This is another obstacle.

Even knowing this, she can barely look at Clarissa and Lauren.

"Hello? Loser much? Where's your book today?" Lauren calls over.

This is ridiculous. What's wrong with reading books? Isn't it better than scrolling through endless dance videos?

"Are you really that bored?" she calls to them.

"What's that?" Clarissa says. "We can't hear you. Could you come a little closer?"

Julie sighs and walks over to them. What does she have to lose, at this point? "I *said*, are you really that bored that you have to try to torture me? What's your problem? I never bother you. I'm just trying to get through the day, like you are."

They look at their nails, newly painted, and roll their eyes at her.

"I'm sorry that I like to read books and that I like my own company. I'm sorry that I don't fit in with your friend group and that I have a hard time being confident enough to strike up a conversation with new people. Wait, hold on, you know what? No! I'm not sorry! I'm not sorry at all, because none of this is your business."

"Oooooh, Jules is getting feisty!" Clarissa nudges Lauren.

"First of all, don't call me Jules. Second of all, yes, I am getting feisty. And I'm going to continue to be feisty, like I learned from my friend Li'l Kimmy, who's a rapper in LA and is way cooler than either of you will ever be."

Wait, did she just say *friend*? That slipped out so easily. Suddenly Julie feels sick. What did she say to Li'l Kimmy? About being unemotional? She was so concerned with getting left behind that she'd said something hurtful to her! Why did she do that?!

"You know what, I've finally figured it out," Julie says to the two of them, crossing her arms. "You're insecure. That's why you're lashing out at me. There's something in your lives that's making you feel bad, and you're taking it out on me so you can make yourselves feel better. But you know what? I feel great. And nothing you say can make me feel bad anymore. I know who I am, and maybe no one likes me, but I like myself, unlike you guys."

Clarissa's and Lauren's eyes widen, and *pop!* They both disappear into nothingness. In their place, a tiny silver puzzle piece hits the ground.

Julie had almost forgotten she was in the maze.

• • •

It's true what he said: Dilip has never felt that smart. He's been told that he's a kinesthetic learner by various teachers, but he always felt like they were just saying that to make him feel better about not doing well on assessments or essays. What does being a kinesthetic learner even mean, anyway? They explained that he learns better through physical movement. This is why his best class is science; they're always moving around, doing experiments, *participating*. But other than that, his grades aren't great.

Yes, he's good at surfing and skating, and he picked up both super quickly, but that doesn't explain how he passed the OVAEO. When one of his surfing friends told him that Onasander had invented some sort of hoverboard that could qualify for a new sport and new form of transportation, Dilip had immediately known he had to *try* to get in. But he couldn't believe it had actually worked. He's sure even the other kids here can tell he's not as smart as they are. And he doesn't have a superpower. He should've stayed behind with Ting-Ting. He's not special either.

But he did see the 108th question, right? Because he knows he didn't cheat.

Anyway, like Julie said, he can barely keep his thoughts straight. Sometimes he feels like a puppy, his mind flitting from one thing to another. It makes him feel out of control and ridiculous. Like even now, as he's walking through this hallway, which is weirdly lined with lockers, he's thinking a million different thoughts instead of focusing on what he *should* be thinking about, which is: Where the heck is he?

He comes to a doorway in the hall. It looks just like his classroom. He can even see the ocean out the window in the distance. He feels happy, even calm for a second, until he sees her. Mrs. Calendari. UGH! His least favorite teacher.

"Dilip! Come in, come in," she says, waving at him from her desk.

Does he have to? It sure looks like it. It's the only open door in the long hallway.

"Hurry up now, Dilip. Stay focused," she says.

He walks in begrudgingly.

"Now, I have an activity I need you to complete today," she says.

She motions to a set of playing cards on her desk. Each card has a different scene painted on it. He realizes they're scenes from the day so far.

"I know this is going to be nearly impossible for you," Mrs. Calendari says, looking stern, "but you're just going to have to try anyway. I know you'll probably fail, but what can I do? The school has asked me to at least give you a shot."

Dilip looks at the cards. There's the turrets of the Institute and Onasander. There's the library and red couches. There's the white room and Edwin doing the math problem. There's the ring of fire and Dilip stepping through it. The cards appear to be matched pairs, with a scene and corresponding action for almost everything that has happened since he arrived at the Institute.

"How did you get all of these?" he asks.

"Don't worry about that. Just focus on the task at hand. Memorize where all of them are, and then I'll turn them facedown. One at a time, you flip one over, then find the corresponding match. I'll give you five minutes to memorize the placements."

Yikes, memorization. Not Dilip's strong suit.

He stares at all the cards in front of him. This day has been so strange. That was to be expected, of course. He knew he'd be going somewhere that no one had ever seen before. But still, this is next level. Why is he doing this now? What is Mrs. Calendari even doing here? He wishes he weren't alone. Edwin would be so much better at this. Julie too, probably. He realizes he misses them. It's a strange feeling. He's never really missed his friends before. Normally, he just sees them when he sees them and doesn't even think about them when they're not around.

"Time's up, Dilip," Mrs. Calendari says.

She flips the cards so they're facedown. The symbol of the Institute—the palm holding the infinity sign—is pictured on the back of each card.

"All right, it's go time. Find the matched pairs."

Dilip takes a deep breath and tries to focus. Mrs. Calendari flips over a card with the Latin riddle. Where was the one with the ring of fire?

He doesn't remember. But he does remember where the one of Julie is. He was staring at it as he thought about their fight.

"Time is ticking, Mr. Aggarwal. I know it's not likely you'll pass this, but you have to at least try so I can tell the principal you did."

He decides to match it with the one of Julie.

"Wrong!" Mrs. Calendari shouts.

"Why?"

"It's not the corresponding one."

"Why not? Julie is the one who spoke the phrase, so it is corresponding."

Mrs. Calendari frowns. "That wasn't in the rule book. . . ."

"What rule book?" Dilip feels emboldened. He flips over two more. This time, they're correct and he knows it.

Mrs. Calendari is taken aback.

"All right, those work," she allows.

He matches more. He's able to remember some, and the ones he doesn't, he knows how to forge a link between them, how to argue their connection. He feels more focused than he has in years.

Mrs. Calendari gives him a rare smile and encourages him to keep going.

Something is clicking for him. Even if he can't win this game by rote memorization, he suddenly feels able to win it by making more abstract connections. Maybe there's more than one way to do well. To be smart. Is that what kines-thetic learning is about?

Eventually, they're all flipped and matched.

He did it!

"Congratulations, Dilip," she says warmly.

Then Mrs. Calendari pops into nothingness. A small silver puzzle piece appears where she was sitting.

Chapter Twenty-Three

UNLOCKING THEMSELVES

It's been a long, long time since Li'l Kimmy's been here: her elementary schoolyard. This place used to be fun. For whatever reason, she'd mostly been friends with boys in elementary school. They'd shoot hoops or make up rhymes. It was the beginning of her interest in rap. They would always freestyle together, though they didn't call it that then. But after sixth grade, the boys had stopped with the rhyming and the rapping. Not Li'l Kimmy, though. She kept it going.

She begins to feel dread, walking toward the greentop. Why is she here? How did she get here? It's as if no time has passed. She sees her friends, three boys, playing around with a basketball. Owen. Pharell. Micah. They're young, like they're back in fourth grade or something. They're ten at most.

"Yo! Eun-Kyung!" Micah calls out. "Over here!"

The name makes her start. None of the Octos have called her by her real name. She walks over.

As she does, Owen throws a basketball at her so forcefully it hits her square in the chest.

"Hey!"

Her friends just laugh and laugh. Now she's starting to remember why they all drifted apart. Those times on the playground weren't so much fun after all. Wow, it's almost like she blocked it out. Seeing their faces again, at this age, brings it back.

"What, are you gonna cry?" Pharell says.

"Crybaby, crybaby!"

"If you want to hang out with us, you can't always be crying, Eun-Kyung!"

She furrows her brow. This is where the chill-girl thing came from, isn't it? All the boys she was hanging out with growing up. Always telling her she was being too sensitive, feeling too much, being such a girl. They said *girl* like it was a bad thing to be.

So she taught herself to be chill—to not let things get to her. At least not in public. What a ton of crap.

"You guys are just the same, aren't you?" she says. "And where are you now? You're probably the same now as you were when you were ten."

"What are you talking about?" Micah says, dribbling the ball.

"We're just having fun, Eun-Kyung. Why do you always have to make everything so heavy?"

"Heavy? You think that just speaking my mind and telling you how I'm feeling is heavy?"

"Whoa, whoa, you're getting kind of emotional!" Pharell says, putting his hands up and backing away. "Have you got your period yet? My older sister gets her period, and I know it can make her really emotional."

"That is so unfair!" Li'l Kimmy says. "Just because I get a period doesn't mean that everything I feel is related to it. That's so belittling!"

"Cranky!" Owen taunts. They all start laughing together. "She's on the rag!"

"C'mon, we're just kidding around," Micah says, still dribbling. "We just don't want you to be so dramatic all the time."

Li'l Kimmy shakes her head in disbelief. She can't believe that she put up with these boys controlling her like this for *years*.

"You know, having emotions isn't a bad thing. Being the cool girl who can hang with the boys is fun, but it puts me in a box! You make it so that I can only exist on *your* terms, and if I show any emotion that you don't think is *chill*, then I'm deemed a loser! But we all have emotions! You do! All of you! Just because you're denying yours doesn't mean I have to do the same!"

The basketball bounces, bounces, bounces . . . then pops into nothing.

A silver puzzle piece clatters to the ground.

Oh!

She picks it up and wishes Dilip were here so she could hand it to him.

Edwin feels, for the first time all day, comfortable. He's sitting at his desk at school. He can feel the weight of his favorite notebook in his hands. All around him, his peers have their chins on their wrists, waiting for class to start.

"Today, kids, we're doing something really special," their teacher says.

Edwin's ears immediately perk up.

"We're going to do a pop quiz, only this time, we'll do it orally, in front of the whole class! If you know the answer, just shout it out."

Excitement buzzes in Edwin's stomach. He *loves* pop quizzes. He was made for pop quizzes. They make him feel *alive*. He always wins at these things. He loves winning. He loves showing off what he knows.

"All right, kids. The first question is: What is the capital of Papua New Guinea?"

That is so easy, Edwin can barely believe it. Obviously, it's Port Moresby. He tries to say it out loud but finds he has no voice. He cannot speak. He tries shouting *Port Moresby*, but nothing comes out. Absolutely nothing.

"No one knows? Okay, no problem, we'll go on to the next one," the teacher says.

Edwin's squirming in his seat, mouthing the words, but his teacher doesn't seem to notice.

"The next question is: Who came up with the theory of relativity?"

Another easy one! Albert Einstein, of course. But once again, he finds he can't say anything.

The feeling is horrible. He wants to give the answer. Pop quizzes have always given him an ego boost. School in general, really, makes him feel good about himself. He always has all the right answers and lets others know that he has them. Without being right, what does he have? But again, when he tries to speak, nothing comes out.

He turns to his classmate, John.

"It's Albert Einstein," he says out of sheer frustration. But wait, words came out!

"Albert Einstein," John says to the teacher.

"Very good, John!"

What?! But it was Edwin who came up with that answer! What's going on? Why is John getting all the credit?

"Now the next question: What is the sixth digit of pi?"

Edwin thinks for a moment. *3.14159 . . . So, nine.*

But again, he can't speak aloud. It's a bizarre feeling, not being able to speak out loud. He wishes he hadn't been able to speak back at the courtyard, when he suggested the girls apologize to each other. That was a silly thing to say. Who does he think he is? They were right about him. This whole time, he's thought of himself as the leader of their group.

But he's not the leader any more than any of them are. Why does he think that way? Why does he feel like he needs to be the one to tell everyone what to do? Is it because he feels like he always needs to take credit for everything?

No one else in the class answers the question. The teacher is waiting. Ah, what the heck—he may as well tell John the answer, even though no one will know it's really Edwin who knew it.

"John. Psst," he says. "It's nine."

John gives him a thumbs-up.

"Nine!" he says.

With that, John turns into a silver puzzle piece before Edwin's very eyes.

Chapter Twenty-Four

FITTING THE PIECES TOGETHER

After the silver puzzle piece appears, so does a door. When Edwin walks through it, he finds himself in a courtyard again with the same tall hedges as before, but it's a different courtyard than the one where they left Ting-Ting. This one has a fountain in the shape of the Octagon Valley Institute symbol, the large hand with the floating infinity sign. And though there's no Ting-Ting, there are three other people.

"Looking for Daedalus?" he calls.

"Theseus is here!" is the answering roar.

Edwin feels a relief so great his knees buckle. He walks farther out of the maze and sees the rest of the group assembled.

"Edwin!" Dilip says, cracking into a smile with deep dimples. "You made it!"

"Thank goodness," Julie says, smiling shyly. The tension from earlier has dissipated between them, and for that they're all grateful.

"How long have you guys been here?" Edwin asks.

"Not long. We literally all just got back, like, just before you," Li'l Kimmy clarifies. "Except Maureen. She's not back yet."

Now the awkwardness sets in.

"Hey, um, about earlier—" Julie starts.

"I think that—" Dilip says at the same time.

They all laugh.

"You go first, Julie," Dilip says.

"I just wanted to apologize," she says. "For before. I didn't mean what I said. I've never really had close friends before. Not that we're friends! I mean, I hope we could be, or we might be, but I mean—um, I'm getting this all wrong . . ."

Li'l Kimmy throws an arm around Julie. "Don't be silly, Jules. Of course we're friends."

"Okay, cool. Nice. I think I just felt scared back there after leaving Harold, Anton, and then Ting-Ting behind. Like, scared that you would do that to me."

"We'd never!" Li'l Kimmy says. "Right, guys?"

Dilip and Edwin both nod.

"And, hello, they all *wanted* to stay behind! We didn't leave them on purpose," she reminds Julie.

"Good point." Julie laughs. "What were you going to say, Dilip?"

"Just that, you know, with my skate friends, I don't really think about them when we're apart. But five minutes away from you guys and I was wishing you were all with me. It was, um, lonely in the maze. I missed my . . . friends." He blushes a bit.

"Not to get too *emotional*"—Li'l Kimmy winks at Julie— "but as crazy as this day has been, I'm glad I'm doing it with the three of you. Plus Maureen, I guess. Where is that girl?"

Edwin clears his throat. "Same. I couldn't do this alone. And, um, I'm sorry, too."

"For what?" Julie wonders. Edwin has been the kindest and most polite of the bunch.

"I dunno, always needing to be right, I guess."

"Well, most of the time you *are* right," Li'l Kimmy says with a laugh. "So you're forgiven."

"Totally," agrees Julie with a big grin.

"Wait, Edwin was wrong on something?" Dilip jokes. "When did that happen?"

"Well, speaking of which," Edwin says shyly, "I think I might have something that will help us out. I found the next piece of the puzzle."

He pulls out the silver puzzle piece. It looks smaller now. "That's weird," he says.

"Wait," Dilip says. "I thought *I* found the puzzle piece for this step."

"Me too!" the girls both say.

The three of them all pull out their puzzle pieces.

"Do these look different from the other ones?"

Dilip pulls out the previous six puzzle pieces from his shorts. They're bigger. Thicker, too.

"So, are these not the right puzzle pieces?"

Julie looks at them more closely. They have some odd grooves in them that the other ones don't. Almost as if . . .

"Wait, what if we put them together?" she suggests.

Li'l Kimmy shrugs. "Worth a try!"

They try several iterations, clicking the puzzle pieces together until finally they find the right placement. The puzzle pieces lock into one single piece and fuse.

"Cool." Edwin stares at the completed piece that's now as big as the others.

Behind them, they hear someone walk through an archway. Julie's heart catches in her throat. Assassins? Murderous sirens? Dinosaurs?

But it's only Maureen, looking bored and disgruntled and carrying a ton of shopping bags.

"So," she says. "What did I miss?"

Chapter Twenty-Five

ONE LAST TEST

"ou okay?" Julie asks Maureen.

"Yeah, why wouldn't I be?" Maureen sneers.

Julie and Li'l Kimmy catch each other's eyes and look to the heavens.

"Did you get one?" Li'l Kimmy wants to know.

"One what?" Maureen asks.

"Puzzle piece?"

Maureen looks confused. "No. I was at some mall for, like, *ever.* Then I got tired of shopping, so I made my way back here. . . . Why?"

"Oh," says Edwin. He thinks about the fused puzzle piece. It was complete. Maureen didn't get a piece, and they didn't need hers anyway. Strange.

"Nothing," Dilip says quickly.

Still, it's weird. The four of them found the four pieces that made up the latest puzzle piece, but nothing's happened. Nothing's changed. No door has appeared. So far, finding a puzzle piece always led to the next obstacle, but the next challenge hasn't presented itself yet.

Li'l Kimmy sits on the rim of the fountain, and the rest of them join her.

Maureen sets her shopping bags down. "Are we trapped in this maze forever?" she demands.

"I hope not," Li'l Kimmy says. "I mean, I don't know about you guys, but I could use a snack."

"Snacks!" says Dilip. He unzips his cargo pocket and pulls out the Hot Cheetos. He opens the bag and passes it around.

Maureen crinkles her nose. "None for me."

"Suit yourself," says Dilip. The rest of the group soon have red fingers. They munch contentedly as they wonder how they're going to get out of their latest predicament.

Dilip crumples the bag and stuffs it back into his pocket. "Okay, I know you're going to think I'm, like, really obsessed with the Minotaur thing, but is it possible that we're in a labyrinth and not a maze?" he asks.

Dilip explains that due to his interest in mythology, he's discovered there's a difference between a maze and a labyrinth, though people often use the terms interchangeably. They may provide a similar idea when used metaphorically, but they are not the same. Mazes have many solutions: You can take many paths to reach the end, and typically a maze is a place you go to enjoy being lost for a while, and then you end up on the other side at the end. A labyrinth, however, only has one solution, which always takes you to the center, and when you get to the center, there's usually something waiting there.

Something good? Maybe. But often something bad. Like the Minotaur, the monster that Theseus found in the center of the labyrinth.

In case you don't have the encyclopedic knowledge of Greek mythology that Dilip does, let us get one thing straight: A Minotaur is a pretty vicious creature that's half man, half bull. You really don't want to meet up with one anywhere, let alone in a labyrinth you can't get out of.

"Maybe we've been going about this the wrong way," Dilip continues. "Trying to get *through* the maze instead of toward the center of the labyrinth."

"We're in a maze within a maze," Li'l Kimmy says. "Or maybe a labyrinth within a labyrinth."

"Or a labyrinth within a maze," Julie says. "Should we split up again?" She suggests it halfheartedly.

"I don't think that's a good idea," Dilip says. "We tried that, and even if one of us does find the exit, do any of us want to go through it alone? We're a team at this point. I personally don't want to try to solve this by myself."

The four of them nod in agreement. Edwin and Julie start talking about probability, and Li'l Kimmy tunes out of that conversation, investigating the fountain for some kind of clue instead. Dilip, meanwhile, has a strange feeling overcoming him. He feels elated at having provided some insight about the labyrinth. A sharp sense of joy, suddenly, amid all the panic. Joy that these people aren't like the friends he's known. They see him. They listen to him. And they care about him. He feels a lifting in his chest. He feels so elated that it feels like he's *really* lifting. Off the ground.

Dilip starts to hop from foot to foot, foot to foot, hoping to get some of his energy out. As he does, he accidentally hops too hard, and floats up five feet in the air.

"Uh, Dilip?" Li'l Kimmy says, staring at him, mouth agape.

"Whoa!" he exclaims, hovering in the air.

"Guess we found out what your power is." Edwin laughs.

"What's going on?!" Dilip says, even as he's grinning widely. He's unstable, trying to balance with nothing to hold him. He flips around, still airborne.

"Looks like you have a little practicing to do," Maureen snickers.

"This is so majorly cool!" Julie yells. "How is this possible?!"

Somehow, possible it is. At least within the walls of the Octagon Valley Institute.

Dilip can fly.

Julie is shocked, but not as shocked as she would have been before she found out that Edwin has the gift of telekinesis, or that Li'l Kimmy can shoot fire from her eyes, or that she herself can control minds with music.

Dilip lands softly back on the ground.

"Well, this explains why you're so good at surfing and skateboarding," Li'l Kimmy says with a laugh.

"Have you ever flown before?" asks Edwin.

"Not really, unless you count tricks on my boards."

"Do it again," Edwin urges.

Dilip bends his knees and jumps. This time, he gets to twenty feet and can see above the hedges. He moves his arms and legs gently, as if he's doing the breaststroke in the ocean, and is flung through the air.

"Wow!" he yells. "This is amazing!"

"Why does everyone have a power except me?" Maureen pouts.

Julie looks sharply at Maureen and wonders the same. "Maybe you're still going to get one," she says to be polite.

"Dilip, come back here for a second!" Edwin yells up to him.

Dilip lands back in the part of the maze where his friends are. "That was so sick," he says.

Edwin turns to Dilip with a grin. "I have an idea. One that I think might get us out of here."

Dilip is so high above the labyrinth that his friends look like tiny ants. The green hedges of the labyrinth go on forever and ever toward the horizon with no end in sight. It's pretty amazing to have a bird's-eye view. Maybe they should call it a Dilip's-eye view! He's enjoying the feeling of flying so much that he keeps getting distracted, thinking of all the best places to fly. *It's a whole other world up here in the air. How is it that no one can ever see this? It seems unfair. All humans should totally be able to fly.*

Focus, Dilip, focus! He's on a mission here. A mission to find the middle of the labyrinth. Which doesn't seem so easy, considering how far it spreads.

Dilip knows that he will be able to tell where the door is by the shape of the hedges around it. The center of the labyrinth is usually circular in shape, whereas the rest of the labyrinth is right angles and sharp lines.

After a few minutes of soaring, Dilip spots a circular pattern in the hedges. He flies over to it and drops himself down. It would be so easy to just slip out the door himself, get away from this whole thing. At one point in the day, if presented with the opportunity, he might have done that. He had no allegiance to these kids this morning, sitting in that room. He felt like they were all try-hards, suck-ups, butt kissers who cared more about getting good grades than experiencing nature or adventure.

But now he actually cares about them. In fact, he *really* cares about them! His *joy* from their friendship is what made him discover he could actually fly in the first place. He's grown very fond of Edwin and his encyclopedic knowledge, Li'l Kimmy and her brash hilarity, Julie and her sensitive depth. Maureen he could take or leave, but sure, he'll throw Maureen in there too. Why not—he's feeling generous.

"I found it!" he yells as he flies back over to his friends, using his arms to propel himself. He wonders if there are different ways to fly, like how he surfed through the black hole. He'll have to experiment. But not now. Now, they're on a mission.

From his Dilip's-eye view, Dilip calls out directions, leading his three—ahem—four friends through the labyrinth all the way to the center. When they reach the arch that brings them into the circular part of the labyrinth, Dilip flies down to stand with them. When he lands, they all hug him and pat him on the back.

"Way to go, Dilip! That was radical!" Li'l Kimmy cries. "You have to teach me how to fly like that."

"If you can teach me the fire thing, I'll totally teach you to fly," he says with a laugh.

"If only I had that under control," Li'l Kimmy sighs.

The five of them stand before a silver door. But this time, there's no puzzle on it, no language to translate, nothing to challenge them. There are, however, indentations on the door. Seven, to be exact.

"The puzzle pieces!" Edwin says. "Dilip, bring them out!"

Dilip unzips his pocket for the precious cargo.

"Huh," says Li'l Kimmy, tracing a finger over the indentations on the door. "Onasander told us at the beginning we had to find eight puzzle pieces. Maybe this leads to the eighth?"

"And maybe this is the end of the obstacles?" Julie says in wonder.

They all feel a wave of relief. This must mean they're about to escape. That maybe, just maybe, their trials are over.

"Well, shall we?" Edwin asks.

"Let's do it." Julie nods.

"What else are we going to do?" says Maureen.

Together, the five kids slot the puzzle pieces into the indentations so that they glow with a blue light.

Dilip pulls a door open once more.

A familiar invisible swooshing force sends them, chest first, through the doorway. They land with a thud under a harsh fluorescent light. As they stand up, eyes adjusting to the brightness, they can't believe what they see. It might be the most shocking scene yet.

They're back in the white waiting room, where it all began.

PART THREE: EXTRA, EXTRA!

Chapter Twenty-Six

BACK TO THE START

They did all that work, traveled through different worlds and planes of reality, fell into a void, got attacked by piranhas, walked through a ring of fire, almost got shredded by assassins, faced their deepest fears in the labyrinth, lost Ting-Ting and Anton and Harold—all so they could end up right where they started? Back in this sterile white room?

"You've got to be kidding me," Li'l Kimmy says, slapping her forehead with her hand.

The room is exactly the same, except it's no longer filled with puzzle-shaped desks but with regular desks arranged in neat rows.

Oh, and Harold is nowhere to be found. Did we mention? *Sayonara*, Harold!

"They seriously need to get better lighting in this room,"

Maureen whines, shielding her eyes from the fluorescent light bulbs. "This is way unflattering."

Edwin's mind is running a mile a minute. What could be the meaning of this? Does this mean they're at the end of the test, or are they stuck in a permanent loop? Did they mess with the labyrinth? Are they in another reality? Or one of the maze worlds?

The gold door to the room that they entered hours and hours ago, at the beginning of this very, very long day, opens a crack. They all freeze. Daphne? Assassins? Ting-Ting? Anton?

Ugh! Is it Harold?

Nope.

A familiar man with wild white hair, wearing a powder-blue three-piece suit and thin-framed aviator glasses tilted slightly askew on his long nose, appears in the doorway.

"Ta-da!" he says, spreading his arms wide and doing jazz hands with a goofy grin. "You did it, Octos!"

Edwin feels a rush of adrenaline—a bolt of fear and a tingle of anticipation. Onasander Octagon, the famous scientist and researcher, once more. The man of mystery, now more mysterious than ever.

"You all made it here in one piece! Well, not all of you, alas. But that's to be expected, I suppose," Onasander says, taking off his aviators to polish them with a silk pocket square. He walks to the front of the room, sits on a desk so he's facing them, and starts swinging his legs.

"You five have really demonstrated quite a lot to me today. Why don't you all take a seat? I'm sure you have a lot of questions."

"What just happened? Are you evil? And was all that real?" Dilip demands.

"Yes, those are the sorts of questions I mean! But sit, sit! We'll get to all that, I promise."

The five of them sit down tentatively. Edwin can't help but be skeptical after everything he's experienced today. Is this another test? What does Onasander want with them now?

"Before we get started, I must apologize. I'm sure that this day has been rather stressful, but I promise you, it was all for good reason," Onasander begins, folding his hands and grinning.

The kids stare at him wordlessly.

"Why do you all seem afraid of me now?" he wonders aloud.

"Uh, because you just put us through a series of life-endangering scenarios?" Li'l Kimmy bursts out.

"Oh, it wasn't really dangerous, Li'l Kimmy!"

"Tell that to Anton and the assassins who carried him away!" Julie shouts.

"No, no. You were never really in danger in those tests. I was watching the whole time. However, I had to make you *feel* like you were in danger in order to see how you would react in certain situations."

"That's just sadistic!" Maureen exclaims.

"I promise there's a very good reason for all this. You just have to trust me."

Edwin, a trusting soul, feels immense waves of relief washing over him. They were never really in danger! Someone was watching them to make sure! This is wonderful news. Why do all the others still look so concerned?

"You are perfectly safe in the Institute," Onasander says, feet still kicking against the desk.

Li'l Kimmy huffs, Julie still has her arms crossed, and Dilip is slouching in his chair. Maureen sits as if at attention. Only Edwin, star pupil, nods at Onasander.

"So, where to begin?" Onasander mulls, putting a fist under his chin. "You'd think I might've rehearsed this bit. You see, I needed to know that you could all work together. There needs to be the right chemistry. And certainly not all eight of you were compatible." Onasander laughs.

Julie gets a jolt at this, remembering the other kids. "What have you done with Anton, Harold, and Ting-Ting?" she exclaims.

"Don't worry, they're all perfectly safe. They're resting right now, and soon they'll be given a quick forgetfulness pass and be sent home with their parents, chock-full of memories of a perfectly lovely weekend." Onasander smiles reassuringly. "They're completely fine and unharmed. Even Harold. Although it was tempting to teach him a lesson. But alas, his father probably would not take kindly to that."

"What's a forgetfulness pass?" Li'l Kimmy asks.

Instead of replying, Onasander claps. "Oh, I have so many fun things to show you! But we'll get to that. I'm sure you all were quite surprised to find that some certain, uh, capabilities came out during the tests, yes?"

They all nod cautiously, except for Maureen.

"Capabilities you didn't think you had, or didn't even know were possible. I myself was very glad to see them. But you see, for these talents to appear, I needed to put you in very difficult situations. These things don't just come out for the first time by themselves. They need a little urging."

Edwin is confused. "But how did you know that we could do that stuff?"

Onasander smiles. "Don't you already know?"

"The one hundred and eighth question," Edwin replies. "Of course."

The kids all look at each other. The 108th question. The one Ting-Ting cheated on. The one Harold didn't see either. Did Anton ever say whether he'd seen it? No one can recall.

"Only an Octo could answer that question."

"What's an Octo?" Dilip inquires.

"What is an Octo, indeed! That is a very good question, Dilip," Onasander says with a chuckle.

Edwin notices Maureen's been quiet this whole time. Which is very unlike her. He turns to look at her and sees her eyes darting around the room quickly.

"You see, Octos are a very special kind of person, and I'd have to start at the very beginning—the Big Bang, as it were. . . ." As Onasander begins to explain, Li'l Kimmy, Dilip, and Julie are rightfully rapt to hear what he'll say next, but Edwin's eyes are still on Maureen. Something's about to happen, he can sense it.

And!

In a flash, Maureen is up. She runs across the small room, pries open the silver door at the other end, and snatches the seven puzzle pieces from their slots in the doorway. She looks right at Onasander.

"I know your secret!" she squeals, unable not to relish whatever victory she thinks she has achieved.

Onasander instantly replies. "Hidden things make the world go 'round."

As he speaks, he takes a step toward her, reaching. But she slams the door quickly behind her.

"What the . . ." Li'l Kimmy rises from her chair.

"Maureen!" Julie shrieks.

Dilip jumps up, Edwin right behind him, and they lunge at the door. Dilip tries to open it, but it's useless.

"She's gone!" he yells.

"Oh dear," Onasander sighs. "I had a bad inkling about her."

"You did?" asks Julie.

"Yes, but I ignored it. She has such pretty hair!"

Li'l Kimmy's jaw drops. "Pretty hair? That's all it takes?" (Sadly, yes.)

"Well, at least she's finally shown her true colors," says Onasander. "Pity about the puzzle pieces, though. We were going to use those."

Chapter Twenty-Seven

YAK WHO?

"How on earth did they manage to recruit her?" Onasander mutters to himself, pacing around the room. "Hmm, this is a quandary. If she's one of them, that means . . . that means they must be close. Maybe they're already here. Egads!"

Seeing the four kids staring at him, his face brightens artificially, and he smiles, turning toward them. Toward the Octos. Whatever that means. Will we ever find out?

Oh, the narrative tension!

"Did this dude just say *egads*?" Dilip whispers to Julie.

"Soooo, anyhoo, slight change of plans," Onasander says. "We sort of needed those seven puzzle pieces, because there was one last task I had to ask of you. One last obstacle, if you will."

Edwin's head is spinning. Where did Maureen just go? Why did she take the puzzle pieces? Who are "they"? And what does that mean, *they're already here*?

"These seven puzzle pieces lead to an eighth one, which itself leads to something that we really need. I suspect it's the same thing that the, uh, visitors are here for. The Impossibilium."

"Impossibilium? What's that?" Edwin asks. It vexes him that he's never heard of it. Should he have heard of it?

"It's a very precious substance. A building block of the universe, if you will. I'll explain more later, but right now, it is imperative that we find it before the, um, visitors do."

"And how will we do that?" Li'l Kimmy wants to know.

"With the puzzle pieces, of course!" Onasander replies with a smile until he remembers that Maureen has stolen them.

"Did you make copies?" asks Dilip. Surely Onasander, with all his smarts, knows to do stuff like back up his hard drive. It only makes sense. Right?

Alas . . .

Onasander looks sheepish. "Um. No. There are no copies. But see, that was the whole point. The puzzle pieces are very complex, encrypted and protected. Which is why you had to go through obstacles to acquire them. The puzzle pieces lead to something that is so precious, so dangerous, that I created safeguards to keep everything hidden and hard to get to. Even *I* don't have easy access to it. I've hidden the

Impossibilium somewhere in the Octagon Valley Institute, and I've given myself a forgetfulness pass so that if I were ever to be captured and forced to disclose its location, even I wouldn't be able to."

Li'l Kimmy's impressed. That is some next-level planning, yo.

"Why do you keep talking about erasing memories? That's not possible," Julie says. "Is it?"

Dilip floats six inches off the floor. "Is this possible?"

Julie tilts her head. "Fair point."

"The only way to find the Impossibilium is to complete a set of tasks very specifically designed to keep people away. Only a very exceptional group of people could complete them," Onasander says, looking meaningfully at the four of them.

"You mean us!" Dilip says, shocked and smiling as he lowers back down to the ground. "He means us!"

"Now, Maureen appears to have stolen the puzzle pieces, which leads me to believe she's working with a very dangerous organization. It's my own fault: I should have spotted it. I knew there was something odd about her demeanor, but she does have a special glimmer. That must be why YAK has taken her under their wing."

Onasander starts pacing again while the kids look askance at each other.

YAK?

What's a YAK?

Large hairy animal native to Tibet?

Vomit?

Or is it an acronym?

Your Annoying Kids?

Yesterday's Armpit Kinks?

Good guesses!

But Onasander doesn't seem to notice their confusion. "There's still hope! There's one more puzzle piece that they *don't* have. Which is good news! The not-so-good news is that I don't know *where* I hid that eighth piece, and we don't have any of the other seven that can lead us there. But somehow, we need to find the eighth one before they do."

Onasander takes a big breath and closes his eyes. "This was not how I imagined things going." He laughs a bit sadly. "I was rather excited to explain everything to you. But it seems that will have to wait a little longer."

"Mr. Octagon?" Edwin asks.

"First of all, please, please, call me Onasander. Don't make me feel so ancient! *Mr. Octagon,*" he says, a look of revulsion on his face. "Yes, Edwin?"

But before Edwin can reply, the roof is blasted off the waiting room.

In a chaotic instant, the fluorescent lights explode with a bang, showering them with sparks and glass, and the ceiling is thrown up into the air, as if it were light as paper. The Octos quickly rush under their desks as the silver door almost blows off its hinges. The ceiling is completely gone, and when Dilip peers up from under the desk, he sees that far, far above where the ceiling used to be, like a hundred feet above, there's another ceiling. It looks industrial, like a warehouse or factory ceiling, with steel bars.

"What the—" Dilip whispers, eyes wide.

"Is this another assessment?" Julie asks. But Onasander was flung off his feet and across the room by the explosion. By the looks of it, he might be unconscious.

"Whoa, this is messed up," Li'l Kimmy says, huddling under her desk.

Dilip walks over to Onasander to see if he's okay. He crouches next to the mad inventor, their so-called mentor. Onasander looks unconscious, but he's breathing, which is a good sign. His glasses are cracked and akimbo on his face. His powder-blue suit has burns and smoke marks all over it.

"Are we supposed to know first aid?" Dilip asks.

They're all remarkably chill for people in a room where the ceiling just blew off. But at this point, it's going to be difficult to faze them. Onasander just confirmed that the danger of the tests isn't real. But then again, Julie thinks, Onasander isn't looking so hot right now. He seems to be bleeding from his head. Julie takes off her hoodie and passes it to Dilip, who holds it to Onasander's head to stop the bleeding.

"You guys, he looks hurt, like, for real," Li'l Kimmy says. "This is so not chill."

Panic starts to mount. This *isn't* an experiment or an evaluation! They're not in a simulated or controlled environment.

The ceiling just blew up.

The door burst open and hurt Onasander.

This is real life.

Which means they're in real danger!

Onasander sits up suddenly, gasping for air. He grips Dilip's forearm as he coughs. "Eep!" he cries, looking down at the smoke stains covering his suit. "Yikes!" he yelps, looking up at the nonexistent ceiling. "RUN! YAK is here!"

Chapter Twenty-Eight

YAKKED!

The silver door that once opened into a void, then the Amazon River, then a maze of hedges, and is somehow still standing after the explosion, now leads them into a massive warehouse. Onasander holds open the door, waiting for all the kids to exit before following.

"Come! This way!" Onasander says, taking off at a jog. "We're in a very dangerous situation."

Where are they running to, exactly? Li'l Kimmy just hopes Onasander knows. She's surprised he's in such good shape, especially for a famous nerd. And how old is he really? He's so sprightly!

They run through a warehouse filled with crates, boxes piled mountains high. Dilip wonders if he can fly that high. Edwin marvels that the whole time they were just in a big warehouse and they never suspected. Julie's just trying to keep up. Cardio is not her strong suit.

They duck behind a large shipping container. Onasander nods to a few clouds of smoke on the perimeter of the warehouse surrounding an open green door, which must be the source of the explosions. Onasander ushers them to stand behind him and puts a finger to his lips, indicating silence. The smoke along the perimeter hangs in dense clouds.

Li'l Kimmy stands behind Julie, with her chin on Julie's shoulder, looking at Onasander. She watches as Onasander pulls something out of the pocket where his silk pocket square is stored.

It looks like a fancy silver fountain pen. But when he clicks the end of it, it expands in length and width, until it's the size of his arm. It flashes all over with pinpricks of multicolored light. He points it toward the clouds of smoke, and it shoots a silver light that dissipates the darkness.

"WHAT—" Li'l Kimmy accidentally yells, and Julie whips around to clamp a hand over Li'l Kimmy's mouth. She raises her eyebrows as if to say, *Girl! Not the time for noise!*

Onasander keeps firing into the smoke. *Pew! Pew! Pew!*

The kids peek out from behind the shipping container and catch a glimpse of shadowy figures emerging from the smoke. Is Onasander shooting at them? And who are those people? Are the assassins back? Wait, no, those "assassins" were working for Onasander.

Figures step out of the smoke—much smaller and less intimidating than anyone had expected, around three feet tall and wearing suits that look like they're made out of tinfoil. Quick as a snake, Onasander strikes, covering the nearest figure in a fizzy static with his silver baton.

The tinfoil soldier is frozen, and shrieks in frustration.

More and more of the short-statured and tinfoil-wearing army appears, and Onasander keeps shooting from behind the shipping container with his laser. The figures wiggle and squirm, trying to free themselves, but it seems like they're largely unhurt. Just stuck.

A pacifist! Edwin thinks. Onasander really is a good guy.

Without taking his eyes off the assailants, Onasander speaks to the Octos. "You all need to get out of here," he says through gritted teeth. "And find that Impossibilium before they do."

"Aren't you coming with us?" Edwin asks, heart pounding. "Where do we go?"

"Get into my laboratory system," Onasander whispers urgently. "The eighth piece must be somewhere in one of labs. You *need* to find that puzzle piece."

"How do we get there?" Julie whispers back.

"It's near the entrance to the Institute. I took you all through there at the beginning."

"But we had blindfolds on. How are we supposed to—" Julie argues.

Onasander puts his hand out behind himself to silence her and get them to back away from the smoke.

Li'l Kimmy notices that the frozen invaders are starting to move against the white static. The tinfoil is acting as some kind of repellent.

"Fiddlesticks! They found the secret! Don't follow me," Onasander says sternly to the four Octos.

He steps out from behind the shipping crate to get a better aim. But just as soon as he does that, he's surrounded by the tiny, tinfoil-wearing assailants.

They start attacking Onasander with their own weapons, which shoot globby, thick strands of green gloop. He tries to wrench away, but he's stuck in a clingy puddle of Jell-O. Or is it slime?

"Oh no!" Julie yells.

Another figure emerges from the cloud of smoke. This one is wearing a tinfoil suit along with a remarkably familiar plaid headband over her smooth brown mane.

"Stupid Octos!" the familiar voice calls. "YAK lives!"

Maureen walks toward them with a triumphant air, a smirk on her face.

"Maureen? What are you doing? Are you with these . . ." Dilip asks. This whole scene feels so absurd that he almost laughs. He doesn't even know what to call their opponents. Toddlers? Preschoolers? Why are they all wearing tinfoil?

"What am I doing?" Maureen mimics in a nasty tone. "Don't you get it? I'm *beating* you! I'm beating the whole Institute! Honestly, Dilip, how you aced the OVAEO, I'll never know."

Julie puts her arm around Dilip as he glances sadly down at his sneakers. "Don't listen to her," she whispers.

"Maureen, stop it," Edwin orders, an edge to his voice. "This makes no sense. Who are you? And who on earth is YAK?"

"Earth! That's a laugh. You know it is, Edwin. Who is YAK? Not who, what. *What* is YAK." She throws her hair over her shoulders. As if!

Li'l Kimmy is beyond annoyed. "Okay, fiiiine, *what* is YAK?! Did you really need us to ask again? We get it, you know something we don't. Can you please just explain whatever this is?" she demands, waving toward the globbed-up form of Onasander and the tiny tinfoil brigade.

But Maureen is clearly savoring her moment. She smiles condescendingly, clasps her hands behind her back, and starts to pace back and forth, just like Onasander did back in the classroom.

"Oh, Octos . . ." she says, as if she wasn't one of them mere moments before. "YAK is an organization, much like the Octagon Valley Institute. You see, there were actually *one hundred and nine* questions on the Octagon Valley Assessment for the Extra-Ordinary. Bet you didn't see *that*, did you?"

Li'l Kimmy is so over Maureen's snideness. "We barely even know what the Octos are, Maureen. Get to the point."

"Well, there were one hundred and nine questions. Even Onasander didn't know that. YAK infiltrated Onasander's system, and they slipped in an extra question. Looks like I was the *only* person to see it."

So, Edwin thinks, it's confirmed. They're on a team of some kind. Onasander's team. And they apparently are up against another team. The YAK team. Is that why Onasander brought them here? To fight against YAK?

"But," Edwin begins, "if that's the case, why did you work with us this whole time? Why were you pretending to collaborate, to be on our side?"

"Yeah, and why are you telling us all this now, if you're supposedly against us?" Julie pipes in.

"Very fair questions." Maureen chuckles. "Well, the first one is easy to answer. I was weeding out the competition. Getting rid of as many of you as I could." She counts on her fingers. "Harold, Anton, Ting-Ting. Although to be honest, it was too easy to get rid of Harold. He was a gimme."

So that's why she kept advocating they leave people behind!

"They were easy to pick off," she says. "You guys, not so much. But no matter. I was learning your weaknesses so I could defeat you later. And I had to get to Onasander. YAK thought it would be much easier if I was part of the three-day weekend. And why am I telling you all this now? Simple. I'm distracting you."

"Distracting us?" Dilip narrows his eyes. "From what?"

Maureen gives a coy smile and a satisfied shrug. Then, as quickly as she came, she disappears into a hole in the warehouse wall that must have been made by the explosions. She turns around and fires her own weapon, clogging up the hole with sticky green gloop.

The four remaining kids look at each other in shock.

The tiny tinfoil army is gone.

So is Onasander.

"You guys," Li'l Kimmy says, stepping into the spot where Onasander stood, covered in Jell-O. "I think we've just been YAK-ed."

Chapter Twenty-Nine

THE FAB FOUR

"And then there were four," Julie says as they stare at the globbed-up hole where Maureen disappeared, along with the YAK army and Onasander.

Edwin feels terrified and exhilarated at the same time, which seems to be par for the course at Octagon Valley. "I think it's time for an official meeting of the Octos," he says, stepping up on a crate.

"Edwin, get down from there, for goodness' sake," Li'l Kimmy says, holding out her hand.

"Oh, right." He takes it and steps down, discouraged. Why did he do that? Why does he always try to be a leader?

"No, no, you're awesome," Li'l Kimmy explains hurriedly, seeing the crestfallen look on his face. "But that box is marked 'DANGEROUS: Do not put weight on top of box.'"

Edwin sees where she's pointing and is so relieved he starts laughing. "After all this, it would be really unfortunate if a mysterious collapsing box was what did me in," he says with a guffaw.

All four of them start laughing, and it feels good. Really good.

"So, you were saying, Edwin?" Dilip asks. "First meeting of the Octos?"

"Did Maureen come up with that name?" Li'l Kimmy asks. "'Cause if she did, I'm not sure I want it."

"But Onasander called us that too, didn't he?" says Dilip.

"He did call us that, from the very beginning," Julie agrees. "Remember, at The Welcome, Etc.? Hmm . . . That means Harold, Ting-Ting, Anton, and Maureen are Octos too, right? I mean, even if half of them didn't see the one hundred and eighth question. I doubt Onasander makes a lot of mistakes. He seems like he does things deliberately."

(We'll let you in on a secret here, reader. Truly that was just a coincidence! Or as some say it, a *coinkidink*!)

"Um, didn't Maureen just declare herself a YAK?" Dilip reminds.

"Right," says Julie.

"But you might be onto something, Jules," says Li'l Kimmy. "Remember his far-reaching plan. How he hid the puzzle pieces to keep the Impossibilium safe."

"There are eight sides of an octagon. And there are eight of us Octos," says Edwin. "Yeah, I don't think it's a coincidence."

(No! It's definitely a coinkidink! Not everything means something, Octos.)

Another huge explosion rocks the building, making all the crates and boxes teeter dangerously.

"Anyway," Edwin says nervously. "Onasander said we have to secure the Impossibilium and make sure YAK doesn't get it."

"Yeah, he said if we find the eighth puzzle piece, that would lead us to it. But we need the seven puzzle pieces to take us to the eighth, and Maureen stole them," Li'l Kimmy says.

"Didn't Onasander say something about looking for the eighth piece in a lab by the entrance?" Dilip says.

"Right, but how exactly do we get there?" Edwin wonders. "Should we go back into the waiting room?"

"Wait—hold on—what about Onasander?" Julie asks. "Shouldn't we try and rescue him from the YAKs?"

Edwin can't believe that the thought didn't occur to him. "Right! We should go after them and see that he's safe."

Dilip shakes his head. "I dunno, guys, he was covered in Jell-O and surrounded by tiny creatures who are in league with Maureen," he says. "He's the smartest man in the world—I think he can take care of himself. He told us to secure the Impossibilium."

"What do you guys think?" Li'l Kimmy asks. "Rescue or secure? Hey, isn't that an anagram?"

"It is! Pretty slick," Dilip says, fist-bumping Li'l Kimmy. "Language Arts for the win!" She laughs.

Julie bites her cuticles. Outside of the orchestra pit, she's not great at making decisions. "Whatever you guys think is best."

Edwin thinks deeply on the problem. On the one hand, their mentor has been abducted by a mysterious enemy. On the other hand, the mysterious enemy is quite . . . well, small, and so far, more irritating than terrifying.

On the *other* other hand, this enemy is here for a precious substance—a *building block of the universe*, Onasander called it—and it's up to the four of them to make sure it doesn't fall into those same mysterious, evil, and tiny hands. At the very least, Maureen of the plaid headband and the snooty opinions should not have it.

It's decided.

"Let's go find the labs."

They'll do what Onasander asked them to do.

"Let's go back to the waiting room and maybe find out what's behind the gold door. Maybe we can retrace our steps back to the entrance and find the lab system," Edwin says.

They walk in the direction of the waiting room, which is now just a small, flimsy box standing about eight feet high in the hundred-foot-high warehouse. It has four white walls, the silver door they just came out of, and the gold door that Onasander had walked through just minutes before.

"Hmm, I don't know how the waiting room is going to lead us anywhere," Julie says. "Look."

The waiting room isn't against a wall of the warehouse; it sits in the middle of it. Julie walks a full circle around the four walls, including behind the wall that has the gold door attached to it. "If this room is in the middle of the warehouse, then the gold door just leads to the warehouse?"

"Oh, Jules, Jules, Jules!" Li'l Kimmy shakes her head. "Don't you realize where we are?"

Julie frowns. "The Octagon Valley Institute?"

"Exactly! Anything could happen here—anything *does* happen here. So let's not count anything out."

Li'l Kimmy skips ahead of them and pops through the silver door that's hanging by its hinges. Julie, Dilip, and Edwin follow her inside.

Now that it has no ceiling, and now that they know it's just a box in the middle of a warehouse, the waiting room feels different. They make their way to the front of the room, where the desks have toppled over.

"Ready?" Dilip asks, a hand on the doorknob.

They nod.

When Dilip opens the gold door, sure enough, it doesn't lead back to the warehouse. It leads somewhere they've never seen before.

Chapter Thirty

LABORATORY OF SECRET DELIGHTS

"Whoa, look at all this stuff," Dilip says as they walk through the golden door and find themselves in yet another large and cavernous space. But instead of a warehouse full of crates and boxes, it's filled with strange and wondrous materials in beakers and glass terrariums. A fifty-foot telescope sits pointed out a massive window that overlooks the mountains and valleys. The green observatory they noticed that morning!

Gosh, that feels so long ago.

Once all four of them are inside, the door becomes translucent, then disappears.

"You were right!" Julie breathes, elbowing Li'l Kimmy.

Li'l Kimmy beams. "Is this a laboratory?" she asks. "To be quite honest, I've never been in a laboratory before. My school isn't exactly well-funded enough to have lab equipment, but I've seen them on TV."

"I have never seen a laboratory like this," Edwin says, walking forward to touch a massive telescope. "I don't even think Harold's private school would have a lab like this."

A spiral staircase in the corner leads up to shelves with thousands of glass bottles filled with plant matter, strange sharp-looking leaves and delicate, exuberant flowers growing out of each bottle. There's scientific equipment mounted from floor to ceiling on all the walls, glass and metal and wood and concrete objects in shapes none of them have ever even seen, all on shelving units that reach fifty feet high. Edwin can't begin to think what they might be for. Planks of metal hover in the air in front of these cases, as if waiting for someone to step on them. In one corner of the room, there's a large circular metal table with several stools around it, and above the table, liquids of various colors float in the air, suspended and sloshing in a wavy motion. In another corner, there are thousands of books, a red armchair, and a large globe.

"Are we in, like, a secret government lair or something?" Dilip asks.

"I don't know about you," Julie says, "but I have a feeling the government does not know about whatever this is."

"Whoa," Li'l Kimmy says, running over to the circular metal table, "check this out!"

She kneels on a stool and brings her hand to touch the floating liquid.

"No!" Edwin cries, rushing over to her.

Li'l Kimmy recoils from the substance.

"What?" she says to Edwin.

"Those could be dangerous! Look, we shouldn't touch anything in here. We don't know what any of this is or what it could do."

Li'l Kimmy sighs and backs away from the swirling neon-green and bright purple liquids backflipping in midair.

"What's the point of being around all this cool stuff if we can't touch it?" she grumbles.

"Maybe you can touch a book, just not . . . those unidentified substances," Edwin concedes. "Plus, we need to get a move on. What if YAK breaks in here?"

"So, if we were Onasander Octagon's eighth puzzle piece, which leads to a precious substance everyone wants even if we don't know what it is or what it does," Dilip says, "where would we be?"

A simple enough question.

"Yeah, and we should find it as fast as we can. I'm still kind of worried about where they took him, even if they are tiny and wrapped in tinfoil and led by annoying Maureen," says Julie. "What if they hurt him?"

"For sure, Maureen isn't a very nice person," Li'l Kimmy agrees.

"Okay, okay, let's think!" says Edwin.

It's more difficult, in some ways, searching for a hidden

puzzle piece than completing tasks where you're just given one at the end.

Julie tries her luck and steps onto one of those metal slats floating in the air. The one she's on has a symbol of a crescent moon on it. As soon as she steps on it, it lifts, and Julie finds herself flying up, up, up to a circular window thirty feet high.

"AH!" Julie shouts.

"Whoa, go, Julie!" Li'l Kimmy calls. "I want to do that!"

"You guys!" Julie cries, peering out the window into another room. "There's, like, a moon rocket in here!" It's four times the size of an airplane, shiny and silver, with the infinity symbol floating above a palm engraved on the side of it.

"Uh, okay, can I go back down now?" she asks the metal slat she's standing on. *How do these things work?*

The slat remains there, hovering by the window. She turns around so she's facing the room, and for a moment her stomach lurches, doing a roller-coaster drop as she realizes she's on a tiny metal slat floating thirty feet in the air.

"How do I get down, you guys?" she calls. From way up here, the room looks even wilder. For one thing, where there should be a ceiling are faint constellations flickering, and is that a shooting star? It's a good thing she's not afraid of heights. Well, she's a normal amount of afraid.

Edwin ponders Julie's predicament. Things that go up

must come down. Law of gravity, and all. Only one way to find out! He steps onto the metal slat with a symbol of a book on it that's positioned by the shelves. It immediately starts rising, and he yelps in surprise at the feeling, even though he kinda knew that was going to happen. He kneels down to grip the edge of the slat and runs his hands around the device. His fingers find a groove. He applies pressure, and the plank slowly floats down.

"Julie! Press the thingy on the side!" he calls.

Dilip checks out the metal slat nearest him. This must be the hoverboard technology that was his reason for coming here in the first place, the reason he wanted to pass the OVAEO. But then he remembers flying in the labyrinth. He doesn't need this technology anymore; he can fly on his own! He pushes off from the concrete floor and hovers in the air for a moment. Then he starts doing the breaststroke and propels himself around, just like he did in the labyrinth.

"Okay, now you're just showing off, Dilip!" Li'l Kimmy teases.

"You don't want a go?" Edwin asks, stepping off the hoverboard.

Li'l Kimmy shakes her head. "Not for me, thanks. My feet stay on the ground."

Julie crouches on her hoverboard and feels around for the return button. She gets a not-unpleasant whirl in her stomach as it lowers swiftly to its original place.

"Jules." Li'l Kimmy runs over once she's back. "Come check this out."

Li'l Kimmy grabs Julie by the hand and brings her over to an area of the room where spiral shelves hold bizarre looking gadgets. "It's like in a spy movie!" Li'l Kimmy squeals. "What are these things?"

Julie picks up a tiny violin. "This is so cute!" she says, showing it to Li'l Kimmy. "What do you think it does?"

"Play music?" Li'l Kimmy laughs.

Edwin and Dilip come over too. "Do you guys think some of this stuff might be helpful for, you know, battle?" Dilip asks.

"Battle?" Li'l Kimmy says, nerves creeping into her voice.

"You know, like, against the YAKs," Dilip replies. "That's probably not the last we've seen of them."

"Who knows?" Julie says. "This violin seems like the right size for them."

They crack up.

She tries out the little violin. It squeals a few horrendous, earsplitting notes.

"Um, I thought you said you were good at that!" Li'l Kimmy jokes.

"Maybe it does something to the YAKs?" Dilip suggests. "Like there's some note in there that only they can hear and it puts them to sleep."

"They're not *dogs*," Edwin admonishes.

"Still, you never know." Julie shrugs and puts the tiny violin in her pocket.

The four inspect the spiral shelves full of strange objects. There are boxes and baubles and rods and pellets and something that looks like a Bubble Wrap onesie. In case someone wanted to ship a baby?

"Should we each take something?" Li'l Kimmy ventures.

Dilip finds a pack with straps on it and two strange orbs on either side.

"Is this a jetpack?" he asks. "Cool."

"Dilip, you can already fly on your own. Do you really need a jetpack?" Julie asks, bumping his arm.

"I dunno," he says. "Maybe this'll make me go really fast." He puts it on his back like a backpack and presses a button. He spurts just a few feet into the air, then crashes to the floor.

"Are you okay?" Edwin asks, helping him up.

"Yeah, fine." Dilip brushes himself off. "I guess it'll take some practice."

Li'l Kimmy spots a pair of wraparound sunglasses with a flame icon on the side. "Oooh! I like the look of these." She puts them on.

"Those are fire, Li'l Kimmy," says Dilip, laughing at his own bad joke.

"Everybody stand back." Li'l Kimmy turns toward a

relatively empty metal wall. She tries to shoot fire out of her eyes, but all she gets is a sputter, like a candle.

"I guess these also take practice," she says, disappointed.

Edwin scans the shelves and finds a small golden object shaped like the infinity sign. It looks just like the one from the Octagon Valley Institute symbol. He takes it in his hand. It lifts up and hovers above his palm.

"Whoa, just like the logo!" Dilip says.

He's right. His own palm has now become the Octagon Valley Institute palm. Edwin smiles. It feels, strangely, natural. He tucks it away.

"Okay, so we've found some cool things that we don't know how to use," says Li'l Kimmy. "But no puzzle piece. So what now?"

"What do you think, Edwin?"

"What, me?" Edwin asks. He scratches his head in the way he does when he gets nervous. Before coming to Octagon Valley, he never thought of himself as a leader. Just the leader of being different, out of place: the leader of the outcasts. But maybe he is that . . . the leader of the outcasts. Why not?

"Yeah, you," says Dilip with an amused smile.

They hear rumbling and a crash in the distance. YAK? It has to be. Doing whatever they can to find that Impossibilium.

Oh dear. Better act fast, Octos.

Edwin closes his eyes and thinks. "Maybe we need to clear an obstacle to find the eighth piece," he says at last. "That's how we found the first seven, right?"

And then there's another crash, much closer this time, and out of nowhere, a gold door appears.

Chapter Thirty-One

HOARDER MUCH?

"Must be a safety setting," Edwin muses as the door disappears behind them. They have walked through and into another lab. There's more crashing and a muffled explosion. "The doors appear for us, but not the YAKs. That's why they're blowing stuff up. They're tunneling through the Institute in order to avoid falling into the Octo maze."

"The Octo maze?" Julie asks as they walk through the next laboratory. This one is much smaller, closer to a normal-sized room, and filled with rows and rows of mirrors of all different sizes and shapes. Some are shattered, some are stained, some are burned, some are crystal clear. They pick their way across, cautiously.

"Yeah, you know—the obstacle course we just went

through," Edwin says. "Remember, Onasander said he made it so it would be almost impossible to get to the, um, Impossibilium, so the maze is part of that defense mechanism."

"Huh," says Julie as she passes a mirror that doesn't show her reflection. The next second, she's inside nothingness once more.

"It's a mirror to the void!" she yelps, just as she feels several hands pull her out of it.

"You okay?" asks Li'l Kimmy. "That was freaky. One moment you were here, the next one . . . whoosh! We just barely caught you in time!"

"Yeah, I'm all right, thanks." Julie's not as freaked out as she was earlier. Falling into a void? Been there, done that.

Now that Julie's been sorted, Edwin and Dilip continue their conversation. "Yeah, I don't think the maze is here just so we could be assessed," Edwin continues. "I think it's also a way to travel through the massive Octagon Valley complex. Get from one spot to another more quickly and easily."

"Easily?!" Dilip and Julie say in incredulous unison.

"Well, maybe not easily," Edwin admits.

Li'l Kimmy reaches her hand out to touch a mirror with a red flickering flame border. Dilip yanks her hand away before she makes contact.

"Don't," he says. "It's probably going to send you to that ring of fire again. Plus, we might need that hand."

"Fine! Sheesh," Li'l Kimmy says, bumping Dilip's arm

and looking at Edwin. "So, you think, like, Onasander uses the maze to get around?"

"Exactly. And his staff of researchers too, I'm sure. I think that he knows exactly how to navigate the maze. He could probably do it with his eyes closed. But if anyone from the outside world were to break into Octagon Valley, they'd be spun in a million circles, or almost eaten by piranhas, or sucked into space, or locked in the waiting room, or maybe there are other rooms we didn't even see."

They hear another crash—loud. Are the YAKs getting closer to them? It definitely sounds like it.

"Hmmm, seems like we don't have much time," Edwin says, "so I'll be brief. The YAKs have probably figured out, through Maureen, that Onasander has created a maze to keep unwanted guests confused and out of his way. So instead of going through the maze, they're just going to cut through to the center because, as we discovered, it's not a maze at all, but a labyrinth." He stops, and his eyes light up. "The lab system is the center of the labyrinth! Of course! That's why the Yaks are blowing up everything, to get in here."

"Because everything that's valuable and important is in his laboratory," adds Li'l Kimmy, nodding.

They've come to the end of the room, and they hear a loud crash, even louder than before.

"Hold on, I've changed my mind about the plan," Edwin says. "I don't see how we're going to find this puzzle piece without Onasander. We could just be wandering around these labs forever."

"Yeah, the place is endless," agrees Li'l Kimmy.

"But how can we find him? Who knows where they've taken him?" Julie unravels her left braid, a sign she's anxious.

Dilip is scouting the place. "You guys, look!" He points to a glop of green goo on the floor. "The YAKs! Maybe they dragged Onasander through here."

"Wait. They've already *been* here? How?" asks Julie.

"Maybe they came through one of the mirrors?" Li'l Kimmy suggests.

There's a sentence she never thought she'd say.

The green streak leads to another gold door. The four of them look at each other.

"Worth a try," says Edwin.

Dilip shrugs and reaches for the handle. Here goes nothing.

The door opens into a warehouse. But this one is even larger and filled with even more crates and boxes. Li'l Kimmy shakes her head in disbelief. How does Onasander have so much stuff to store? Hoarder much?

"This room's as big as the Grand Canyon!" Li'l Kimmy whispers. "How are we supposed to find Onasander in this mess?"

The Octos slip stealthily into the warehouse. The door

shuts behind them and disappears. As they tiptoe their way from behind one stack of crates to another, a loud crashing noise shakes the entire warehouse. Falling crates! That's what the noise is. The YAKs seem to be causing chaos, knocking over whatever they can.

Edwin silently points to a spot behind another shipping container, next to a ten-story-tall stack of wooden crates. He waves at the other Octos, and they all creep over. But as they're halfway there, another crash interrupts them. This time, way closer. Another crash, just a few crates away.

Then . . .

Edwin, Li'l Kimmy, and Dilip stare in horror as the ten-story stack of crates right in front of them teeters back and forth, back and forth, until the weight of it is too much, and it crashes like a tower of building blocks struck down by a toddler, or, um, a YAK—right on top of their heads!

Three of them scream and put their arms up over their faces instinctively, as if that would do any good. Li'l Kimmy feels tears stream down her cheeks instantly, knowing that she's about to die. It's all so quick they don't have time to react, let alone run away. The crates are so massive, there's no chance they could get out of the way fast enough.

But one of them isn't screaming.

One of them knows exactly what to do.

Out of nowhere, the crates explode in midair. Before hitting the Octos, before tumbling down on top of them, crushing them into little genius bits, the boxes simply splinter to pieces, raining debris all around them. The tiny slivers of wood hitting the concrete floor sound like a million butterfly wings flapping.

Then . . . silence.

Li'l Kimmy, arms still held defensively over her head, opens her eyes.

Julie stands poised with her chin on a tiny violin, her left hand holding the neck and her right hand holding a tiny bow.

"Julie, what did you do?" Dilip says, still in a wincing pose from anticipating impact.

"I don't know," Julie says, dropping her arms from playing position. "When I saw the crates teetering, I just started playing. It just happened."

"Is that what you took from the first lab?" Edwin says, walking closer to Julie to check out the tiny instrument.

"Yeah, it turns sound waves into a weapon or something." Julie shrugs. "I can't believe it! When I tested it back in the lab, it just sounded bad."

The four burst out laughing in relief and disbelief, tears still wet on their cheeks.

"What song did you play, Julie?" Dilip asks.

But before she can answer, a bloodcurdling scream pierces the air.

Chapter Thirty-Two

MORE IMPOSSIBLE TASKS

nasander!

Oh no! It's got to be him, screaming like that. Who else? He's being tortured! Or killed! By tiny little toddlers in aluminum foil. *Snicker.*

"Where is it coming from? Can you tell?" Edwin asks.

Dilip shakes his head. "This place is too big. It could be coming from anywhere."

They would never be able to live with themselves if Onasander came to harm. Sure, he wanted them to secure the Impossibilium, but what is an unknown powerful and mysterious substance compared to the life of a human being? They should have gone after him immediately!

"We've got to hurry!" says Julie.

"Dude, we *are* hurrying!" stresses Li'l Kimmy.

"I think it's this way," says Edwin. "Let's go!"

Dilip has never felt so much adrenaline in his life, not even when he surfed that monster wave in Hawaii last spring break. His mind is swirling, but there's been no time to stop and process what's happened. This morning he was just a regular kid from California. And now he's not so sure. Things are turning out to be much more complicated than they once seemed. But one thing he does know is that he can't just let someone suffer. Not if he can do something about it. Which is kind of a cool thing to know about himself. Go, Dilip!

"Do the YAKs know we're here?" Li'l Kimmy whispers. "Did they throw those crates at us?"

"No, I think that was just a happy accident for them," Julie answers. "It seems like the crates falling was a byproduct of whatever they're doing in here."

Dilip is right behind Edwin, who leads them through the fallen stacks of crates and boxes to the opposite side of the warehouse.

As they quickly make their way over, Julie notices crates with strange labels on them. UNLIKELY THAT THIS IS WHAT YOU'RE LOOKING FOR, one has written all over it in black sharpie. A few meters to the right, another is covered in red tape that reads HALF-BAKED ANSWERS IN HERE. Julie tugs on Li'l Kimmy's sleeve and points at it. Li'l Kimmy's eyes widen, and then she spots another one a few paces ahead, shoved onto a metal shelf. It says WRONG ANSWERS ONLY on yellow caution tape, next to another one that says TURN AROUND THREE TIMES, GO TO THE LEFT, AND SEE WHAT'S THERE.

As they giggle at the labels, Edwin motions for them to come close, hide behind a stack of crates, and be quiet. He shakes his head at them, upset.

Julie peers over Dilip's shoulder and sees, to her horror, about ten yards away, the one and only Onasander Octagon, genius, inventor, mentor, and founder of this here Institute, standing in the middle of a group of tinfoil-wearing YAKs, two YAKs holding his arms.

Onasander is trying to point despite having his arms held by YAKs. He looks completely exasperated and not at all frightened. More importantly, aside from the minor wound on his forehead, he looks relatively unharmed.

The four kids are all greatly relieved to see this. He's pointing to a crate at the bottom of an absurdly tall stack, even taller than the stack that Julie exploded.

The bloodcurdling scream returns. This time they can see that it's *not* Onasander emitting this earsplitting noise, but one of the YAKs who is particularly frustrated. Said YAK is pulling on his hair and stomping his feet. The other YAKs seem to be equally frustrated, scratching their heads and chattering away about how best to get out the crate that Onasander indicated.

The main YAK is totally having a temper tantrum.

Onasander looks bored, like a parent attempting to placate a toddler. (Which is how big these YAKs are, remember.)

"I have an idea. I might be able to distract them so we can get Onasander away from them," Li'l Kimmy says.

Julie, Dilip, and Edwin look at each other like *Are we sure?* So far, Li'l Kimmy's confidence has gotten her far, but sometimes Edwin wonders if she doesn't totally think things through. Are her instincts good? No time to wonder, because she's already stepping out from their hiding place and into the sightline of the YAKs.

Does she know what she's doing? Not exactly. Does she know how these weird glasses she swiped from the lab work? Not at all. But there's one thing she knows how to do well—a thing that being the chill girl has taught her, that rap has taught her.

She knows how to freestyle. She can make it up! Go with the flow!

The headset does have a sort of video-game feel to it when she puts it on. In her line of vision, numbers and arrows appear. Through the screen, she sees the YAKs, who—luckily—haven't noticed her. The arrows, she realizes, are made of little fire symbols. Then letters flash at the top of her vision.

AIM HERE. AIM HERE. AIM HERE.

FOR DIRECT LINE OF FIRE, AIM HERE.

FOR WALL OF FIRE, AIM HERE.

Li'l Kimmy doesn't want to hurt the YAKs, but she definitely wants to *scare* them.

Behind her, Julie is freaking out, holding her breath. Somehow, the YAKs are too distracted by whatever's in the crate to see Li'l Kimmy, but she's sure that any second now, they're going to see her and cover her in green goop. She can't afford to get YAK-ed. She hates Jell-O!

The thought of Jell-O makes her nauseated. Her aunt made a Jell-O "salad" once, which was a Jell-O mold and inside it was—she kids you not—cottage cheese, nuts, and raisins. The thought of it still makes her stomach turn. But her aunt said it was an American delicacy!

Pushing the Jell-O "salad" out of her mind, Li'l Kimmy takes aim. A thin veil of fire surges continuously from her eyes. The YAKs are on one side of the fire and Onasander is on the other. Only the two tiny YAKs holding on to his arms are still with him.

Unlike earlier by the river, Li'l Kimmy's control is . . . awesome.

"Get Onasander!" Li'l Kimmy yells at the Octos.

Without missing a beat, Dilip, Julie, and Edwin run to the left of Li'l Kimmy's fire wall, where Onasander and his captors are. Dilip and Julie tackle the YAKs who are restraining Onasander, sending the whole group tumbling.

Edwin helps Onasander to his feet. As soon as he does, the two YAKs run for their lives.

"Let's go!" Dilip yells, and the Octos—and Onasander—run in the other direction.

Li'l Kimmy takes the rear, walking backward, keeping the fire shield in front of her while her friends run away through the warehouse. The YAKs keep their distance. This headset is really doing wonders!

"Onasander," Edwin huffs, "where should we go?"

In his scuffed-up powder-blue suit, Onasander stops halfway through the warehouse. He pauses and holds out his hand, touching thin air. He touches the air in a sequence, like doing a handshake with someone invisible. Out of nothing, a door appears, at first translucent, then firming up quickly.

"How the—" Dilip starts, shocked. But he doesn't finish his sentence. At this point, there is such an onslaught of seemingly impossible things flowing toward him, it's best to just surf them.

Onasander pulls on the handle and opens it to reveal a small white room. "Get in," he says.

The Octos file in one after another through the doorway hanging in the air. Li'l Kimmy is the last one through, extinguishing her fire as she steps inside.

"Another waiting room?" Li'l Kimmy says.

Onasander closes the door behind them. The room has them all feeling claustrophobic. It's tiny, just big enough for them all to stand in. It's bright, but the light seems to be emanating from the walls themselves. It's an empty room, completely blank. Like being inside a piece of paper.

Onasander releases a frustrated breath and pulls at his wild white hair.

"You fools!" he says.

Chapter Thirty-Three

THE MOST IMPOSSIBLE TASK OF ALL

Fools? This was not the warm, grateful response that Edwin had been hoping for.

"Excuse me," Dilip says, arms crossed. "Did you just call us fools after we *rescued* you?"

Onasander releases a deep sigh and rubs his eyebrows. "I'm sorry, Dilip, I didn't mean to call you fools. You're absolutely nothing of the sort. In fact, you're the opposite of fools, which is why you're a part of this whole endeavor in the first place. But I had hoped you would understand how important it was to secure the Impossibilium. I was quite safe. YAKs are tenacious, but easily bamboozled. I'd just point to a crate on the bottom of a large stack, telling them that's where it was, and they'd spend hours removing every crate on top of it only to find there was nothing inside the box other than a military-grade aquatic hovercraft."

Li'l Kimmy blinks. "Dude, can I get a ride in that?"

"Of course, of course, another time." Onasander pats her shoulder congenially.

Even amid all the chaos, Edwin and Julie can't help but crack a smile that Li'l Kimmy just called Onasander Octagon *dude.*

"Can we get back to the YAKs?" Edwin says. "How in the world would we know you didn't need rescuing from them? We talked to you for approximately three seconds before the room exploded!"

"Well, did you at least find the eighth puzzle piece?" Onasander asks, exasperated.

The four Octos shake their heads, ashamed.

"I don't suppose it could be in here?" Julie asks.

"Sadly, no. We're the only things that can fit in here," says Onasander.

"Where even *are* we?" asks Li'l Kimmy.

Onasander smooths his suit lapels. "This is what I like to call an emergency hatch. Little invention of mine from a few years ago. Bending space to pop an emergency room in, which is only accessible by me. Essentially, you're ripping space open and stepping inside a secret part of it."

Li'l Kimmy's head is spinning trying to follow along with this, but Edwin is nodding enthusiastically.

"Incredible!" he says. "Can you teach us how to do that?"

"All in due time, Edwin. First, we have more pressing matters to attend to. Again." Onasander takes a deep breath. "I realize that this might be a bit of a strange day for you all," he says.

Dilip bursts into laughter. "To say the least."

"I know, Dilip." Onasander smiles. "You have a lot of new information to take in. And I promise, I will explain everything. But right now, there's not enough time. Beginning to tell you about everything would just inspire more questions, and frankly we don't have the time or space to get into all of it. Ha. First things first: YAK has been after the Impossibilium for a long time."

Onasander runs his fingers through his wild hair. "Now, I can be a bit, uh, shall we say, absentminded at times. I'm aware it's not one of my better qualities. When YAK arrived, I thought I would lead them on a wild-goose chase around the warehouse. I was hoping that while I led them on this chase, you would rescue the Impossibilium."

"So you got caught on purpose?" Edwin asks.

"Precisely. Now, given what information you had, rescuing me the way you did was in fact the correct, not to mention compassionate, solution. Great job controlling your fire, by the way, Li'l Kimmy. I've always wanted to see those glasses in action, but I've never had anyone with the proper power to use them."

Li'l Kimmy smiles, gratified by the compliment.

"So, right! Back to the plan. We must find the eighth puzzle piece, which will lead us to the Impossibilium. Make sure YAK doesn't get their hands on it, whatever the cost."

"What will happen if they do?" Edwin asks softly.

"Trust me—you don't want to know. It's terrible." Onasander says. "Do you trust me?"

It's a good question. Do they trust this man who locked them in a small white room, threw them into a maze that they didn't even realize was a maze (and is actually a labyrinth), plopped them in the middle of a piranha-infested river, sent assassins after them, made them walk through a ring of fire, didn't reveal anything to them for the longest time, and won't reveal things to them still?

Will they trust this man who clearly has so many secrets? This man who, for better or for worse, has provided them with a more exhilarating day than any of them have ever experienced?

The Octos look at each other. Of all the challenges they've faced today, this is by far the hardest. But against their better judgment, they nod.

"Splendid answer. Now, to my lab!"

Chapter Thirty-Four

ELEMENTAL SCIENCE

But which lab? That is the question. Onasander seems to be in possession of an ever-unfolding reality. It's so unlike the reality that Dilip was familiar with before entering Octagon Valley, where the rules were the rules. Here, the rules seem to be ever shifting, or if not shifting, then ever revealing themselves. The Octagon Valley Institute is not a normal kind of building; that became obvious to the Octos long ago. Nor is it a normal kind of institute. Though, to be fair, Dilip isn't sure exactly what a normal kind of institute is like. Has he ever been to an institute? Not that he can recall. He is quite sure, however, that normal institutes don't have sirens swimming around, or mysterious mirror rooms, or laboratories full of floating liquids. What do they normally have? Chalkboards? Whiteboards? Smartboards? Octagon

Valley doesn't seem to have any boards, except if you count the silver door where Julie solved the math problem.

Onasander opens the hatch, and they all step out one at a time into a room that's basically an aquarium, with a long hallway between two glass walls full of aquatic life.

"How do we keep getting transported from place to place?" Edwin asks. It's been on his mind ever since they got here. "How can all this be possible?"

"It's an incredibly advanced technology that you can systematically code to shift the reality of space. Well, at least how space is organized through portals."

"Cool," says Edwin.

"I'll teach you when this is over," Onasander promises.

"Onasander, I have to ask you something," Julie says. "I've read online that your most interesting work is all top secret, never revealed to the public until it's ready."

"I read that too!" Edwin chimes in.

"Is that what the labs are for? The top secret experiments?"

"Something like that," Onasander says, maddeningly mysterious as always. Does this guy ever answer a question directly?

When they come to the end of the hallway, he turns the doorknob left, right, left, left, right again. He opens the door and leads them into a room with blindingly bright sunlight.

The room is full of plants, and there doesn't appear to be a ceiling. Though, as Edwin squints, looking up, he thinks he can see a reflection of glass hundreds of feet in the air. So perhaps there is a ceiling, just far, far above. So far you can't even see it. What a metaphor.

Onasander leads the Octos down a stone pathway that snakes through the large room. "This is my greenhouse, by the way," he says. "There are some very, very powerful plants in here. The world of flora is such a wonder."

The room is full of trees and bushes of all varieties. Pines, oaks, palms. Trees with swirly trunks that twist around each other, trees that grow sideways, trees with neon-green leaves and big juicy fruits. The same fruits in the orchards outside! Edwin doesn't understand how trees that survive in such different climates can all coexist here. Then there are the flowers, massive and bursting with color, rows and rows of them. Also, many plants the likes of which Edwin has never seen. Curlicues, polka-dotted plants, plants with tiger stripes, plants that seem to have jaws opening and closing. He recognizes a few leaves from the first laboratory they were in. This must be where those plant clippings came from.

"Let's take a pause and breathe in the fresh air, shall we?" Onasander says.

It seems like a strange thing to do, given that they're running against the YAK-shaped clock, but Onasander seems to know what he's doing.

At least, sort of.

Onasander leads them off the stone path and into the vegetation of the greenhouse. They come to a little clearing.

"This is one of my favorite meditation spots in all of Octagon Valley," Onasander says serenely. "The other is in the solar system room. Something about bobbing between the planets really puts things in perspective. . . ."

He motions to the ever-astounded Octos to take a seat. There are several plants growing in a circle. The plants have stems so thick they look more like bright green trunks. They each have one large, thick leaf that hovers about a foot off the ground in a crescent moon shape. Onasander sits in the dip of one of the giant leaves, and the plant bobs gently but supportively under his weight. Julie is amazed. She's never seen such a thing.

"Please, take a seat!" Onasander says, motioning to the plants.

The Octos all sit and bounce gently in their leaves.

"Nature is a wonder, isn't it?" Onasander says. "We must never take it for granted. It's the most magnificent science of all." He takes another deep breath. "Yes, I think it's the right time to explain how we got here. First—what exactly is Impossibilium?"

Julie sinks into a palm frond. Sitting down feels so good, she realizes it's been hours since she's sat down.

"Who can tell me how many known elements there are in the universe?" Onasander asks.

"One hundred and eighteen," the four Octos all say at once.

"Wonderful. So here's the thing about Impossibilium.

It's a rare substance. Very rare. So rare that it doesn't exist on Earth. Otherwise known as an alien substance."

Edwin's skin starts to tingle.

"The YAKs believe that they can use this otherworldly substance, Impossibilium, to create a new element," Onasander continues. "The one hundred and nineteenth element."

Onasander lets that sink in.

"And then what?" Edwin asks. "What will they do with it?"

Onasander stands up suddenly. "Time to keep moving, Octos."

Typical, Dilip thinks. *Just when you think you're really getting somewhere in understanding the Octagon Valley Institute, things keep on moving.*

Chapter Thirty-Five

MULTIPLICATIONS AND MULTIPLES

As they reach the far end of the greenhouse room, Onasander turns the doorknob in a sequence of lefts and rights once more. Though Onasander still refuses to explain exactly what's going on with the space-bending, portal-hopping practice, Julie is starting to think it has something to do with how one turns the doorknobs.

The door opens to a familiar room. It's the main laboratory—the one with the massive telescope, the spiral gadget shelves, the library wall, the hovering liquids, and the rows of plant cuttings in glass bottles.

"Thank goodness everything is all still here!" breathes Julie. "I'd hate to see the YAKs destroy this place."

"I take it you've all been here before?"

Edwin nods. "We found this room after leaving the waiting room in the warehouse, when you were captured."

"Very good, Octos." Onasander nods. "Exactly as I told you to."

Onasander walks to a plush red armchair by the library section of the lab and takes a seat. It rises up in the air, hovering gently.

"Now, I have a feeling that the eighth puzzle piece is in this room. Of course, I don't know for certain after my forgetfulness pass."

"What the heck is a forgetfulness pass, already?" Dilip implores.

"Oh goodness, did I not tell you?" Onasander exclaims as he floats around on his chair. "I can be so all over the place, can't I? A forgetfulness pass is a little trick I invented. It's a serum, actually made from the DNA of one of the flowers you saw in the garden, that can perform a targeted amnesia. Surprisingly helpful, but of course, very dangerous in the wrong hands. As most things are."

The Octos think of all the implications a "trick" like this might have.

"But back to the puzzle piece. If I know myself, which I like to think that I do, then I believe that I would have chosen this room to hide it in. For one, it's the most difficult room to enter, since you more or less have to have my permission to enter it. And for two, it has the most hidey-holes."

"How did we enter the room earlier, if we had to have your permission?" Li'l Kimmy asks.

"I have a controller, you see." Onasander removes from his pocket a smooth flat circular thing that looks like a glass rock. He gives it a few taps, and lights of different colors beams through it.

"I like to be able to communicate with my architecture," he says. "This allowed me to grant you permission to enter."

"I know this is a little off topic, but I've been wondering something, Onasander. What does it look like? The Impossibilium," Julie asks, standing near the giant telescope. Outside, the sun is beginning to set.

"Great question, Julie," Onasander responds. "Unfortunately, like a few of the one hundred and eighteen elements, it's a substance that is undetectable to the eye."

"Oh man!" Dilip whines. "You've got to be kidding me. How can we find it, then?"

"Like most things that are undetectable, it's hidden in something you can, um, detect. But as to what that is, I've forgotten." Onasander shrugs. "For its safety, and the safety of the multiverse. But first—the puzzle piece. Hmm . . . where could it be?"

Dilip says he'll take the floating liquids. Maybe the puzzle piece was made to float. Julie goes for the plant clippings. Li'l Kimmy volunteers to plunder the science equipment.

"What about you, Edwin?" Julie asks.

"I'm still thinking," he says.

There's an itch at the back of his mind that if he could just scratch . . .

Then an idea hits him. What if he can use the same power that allowed him to move the desks with his mind to move the eighth puzzle piece toward him?! How had he not thought of this before?!

As the other Octos start their searches, Edwin closes his eyes and concentrates. He thinks of the eighth puzzle piece and tries to draw it toward him, the way he did with the desks, envisioning it clearly. But that's just the problem. He can't envision it because he doesn't know exactly what it looks like. He pictures it like the other puzzle pieces, but nothing happens.

No cigar, kiddo. But good try.

He opens his eyes and tries not to look discouraged. Thankfully, Dilip starts asking a question, distracting him and the others.

"So, Onasander," Dilip asks as he takes a seat at the metal table, "what's so dangerous about the one hundred and nineteenth element that it's made you work so hard to keep the Impossibilium away from the YAKs?"

"YAK," Onasander clarifies. "Like COBRA or SPECTRE or VILE, which if you've watched television or movies, you understand."

"You mean it's an acronym for a totally evil organization," says Edwin.

"Evil?" Onasander ponders. "Not sure if they're evil so much as misguided. Sure, they might have some malicious intent, but for the most part YAK is . . ."

A giant hairy animal commonly found in Tibet?

A puddle of vomit?

The kids wait with bated breath.

"YAK is YAK," says Onasander. He sighs deeply and leans back in the armchair. "YAK already attempted to make the one hundred and nineteenth element once, using Impossibilium. They destroyed an entire reality."

Dilip, Li'l Kimmy, and Julie's heads all snap up from their respective searches. Did he just say it destroyed a reality?

"What do you mean 'destroyed a reality'?" Julie asks.

"I mean just what I say," Onasander replies. "Oh, perhaps I forgot to explain that part. We live in a multiverse, you know. Thank goodness for that, am I right?" He starts laughing heartily, clenching his belly and heaving. He wipes a tear from his eye. "A little multiverse humor, I suppose. Yes! We live in a multiverse, my Octos. Isn't it wonderful?"

"So, Dilip's theory about the labyrinth . . ." Edwin says, swiveling to Dilip.

"Yes," Onasander says. "Together with your theory about the multiverse, I've designed a labyrinth that's able to transport the traveler between multiverse dimensions. Of course, it's completely random, as you know by now, which dimension you enter. That's why it's so dangerous. Which is quite effective when trying to stave off thieves like YAK!"

"So we actually *were* in danger in the labyrinth?" Li'l Kimmy asks, eyes widening. "I thought you said that we were never in danger!"

"Never any *real* danger, Li'l Kimmy. I would have dropped in to rescue you if anything went truly awry. Fear not. Plus, I knew by then that you could handle it. Besides, you had to enter the labyrinth to find the puzzle pieces to prove that you are worthy of being Octos. So."

He shrugs, as if to say, *No big deal.*

"So, what happened when one of the realities was destroyed?" Edwin asks.

"Well, as you can imagine, wiping out a reality in a multiverse is awful for that reality's occupants, of course, as they're completely obliterated, but it also sends shock waves through the whole multiverse. The reality that was destroyed was quite close to ours. Some people say you can still feel the shock waves in our reality. It's caused our reality to, um, be a little vulnerable."

As Onasander finishes saying this, the entire room shakes.

"Is that a shock wave now?" Li'l Kimmy asks.

"No, I think not," Onasander says, shaking his head. "It's YAK."

Chapter Thirty-Six

THE EIGHTH PIECE

All this talk of realities, worlds, and multiverses triggers something in Edwin. Another earthquake rumbles through the room, making all the variously colored liquids in the beakers jiggle and the palm trees shake.

"Right, no more time for talk," Onasander says. "If we can't find the puzzle piece or the Impossibilium, we'll just have to move on without them. I wouldn't trade your lives to find them. Even if the waiver your parents signed upon your acceptance exempts me from any legal responsibility there."

"Really?" Li'l Kimmy goggles. "Moving on without it doesn't seem like a real option. What if YAK destroys another reality? Like, *our* reality?"

"We'll just have to hope that the Impossibilium is well hidden," Onasander sighs.

"Weak sauce!" Li'l Kimmy shakes her head. "No way, we've got to find it!"

Hidden. Reality. No, that's not quite it. The itch at the back of Edwin's mind is getting stronger.

"Where in the world is this thing?!" Dilip cries out.

World! Hidden . . . world. The itch is growing nearly unbearable. At last, Edwin scratches it.

"Hidden things make the world go 'round!" he exclaims.

"What's that, Edwin?" Onasander asks.

"That's what you said to Maureen when she said she knew your secret. I thought it was so strange. Someone tells you they know your secret, and you respond with 'hidden things make the world go 'round'? But it was a code!" Edwin cries gleefully.

"Code for what?" Julie asks, following Edwin as he walks over to the library corner.

He picks up the globe prominently displayed on the shelf and smashes it on the ground.

"Careful!" Onasander shouts.

The globe explodes, shattering in pieces across the floor. Countries, continents, oceans, all ruptured. But from inside the globe, a silver ball rolls across the floor. Edwin picks it up.

The eighth puzzle piece.

"Well done, Edwin. Well done!" Onasander gives Edwin a pat on the back. The other three Octos cheer.

"Okay, so what now?" asks Edwin, staring at the silver orb.

"Oh dear, this is when the other seven pieces would have been helpful," frets Onasander.

"Why?" asks Edwin, then he realizes he knows the answer. "Because it's a map. The puzzle pieces form a map to the Impossibilium!" he shouts in excitement.

He stares at the silver orb in his hands and closes his eyes, remembering what the other puzzle pieces looked like when they were clicked into the indentations on the door that led them out of the labyrinth.

"He has a photographic memory, remember?" Julie whispers.

In his mind, Edwin can see the seven pieces making a circular shape with a hollow center. That must be where the eighth piece goes. There's a line on each of the puzzle pieces that leads to the middle. It's a map of the Institute's maze. Edwin smiles, eyes still closed. "I can see the line. The blue line."

"Good, good, Edwin," Onasander says softly. "Where does the line lead?"

"It looks like it shows what direction to walk in. . . ."

Put together, the puzzle pieces would create a map of the Octagon Valley Institute. He can see the path that they took out of the bright white room, dropping down into the river, then to the left riverbank, and following along until they hit the tree trunk with the riddle on it. The puzzle piece that is the composite of their four smaller pieces has lines in all directions, presumably showing the paths all of them walked in to get here.

But then there's the last one. The one he's holding now. The eighth puzzle piece has a swirling pattern on it.

"What does this swirling mean?" he asks aloud, looking at the orb in his hands.

Could it mean just going in circles and circles? In the very center of the swirl is a small wave icon. The other pieces mapped out the direction they took in a horizontal line, so what can this mean? Because, Edwin thinks, that's what lines mean. Horizontal movement. But they didn't just move horizontally, did they? So how would a map like this show vertical movement?

"The swirl," he says in awe. "I think it means to move up or down. And there's a wave in the center. What could that mean?"

Onasander's eyes light up with recognition. "Oh, Onasander, you sneaky fellow," he says to himself. "I know just where it is. And who I left it with."

The four kids get a shiver of excitement.

"But before we go, I have something I want to give you," Onasander says.

Onasander walks over to the spiral shelf full of gadgets. He fumbles around but doesn't find what he's looking for.

He turns back to them, and it's as if he's noticed them for the first time.

"Ah, good, so you each found your gifts, not just Li'l Kimmy," he says.

"Can I ask," Dilip says shyly, "what mine does?" He motions to the object he's been wearing strapped to his back. "Is it a jetpack?"

It does have the appearance of a jetpack, though none of them have ever actually seen a jetpack in real life.

"Not quite." Onasander smiles. "Jetpacks have been around since the 1940s, you know. It's more like a mini space suit. Rather than taking you up in flight, this is meant to *help* you fly. It'll help you fly higher and faster than you ever thought possible."

"That won't be hard," Dilip admits, "since I never thought any of it was possible."

"Right. To the Impossibilium!" Onasander points to several silver platforms with a wave symbol engraved on them and they each step on one. They ride their silver platforms up, up, following Onasander to the ceiling of his study, where a door hangs in midair. Onasander opens it, and when they step through, they find themselves above a massive lagoon.

"Where are we?" Li'l Kimmy says in awe, taking in the turquoise waters.

"A different vantage point can do wonders for the imagination, can't it?" Onasander says, smiling.

"Is this the aquarium?" Dilip asks.

"I wouldn't call it an aquarium, Dilip," Onasander says with a chuckle. "That implies the creatures within it are in captivity. That's very much not the case here. They're not being kept in captivity, nor are they oddities to stare at. They're conducting research of their own. In fact, one of my top collaborators, Daphne, is here. You might remember her."

"Daphne?" Dilip asks, struck. "You mean the siren from the maze?"

"Indeed, I did ask her to help play a role in the maze. But now I realize that after wiping my memory, I may have asked her for too much!"

Onasander walks over to a rock at the edge of the lagoon and sits. There's an enchanting, moonlit quality to the light. As if they've stepped into a fairy tale.

The four of them stand a few paces back from Onasander, waiting and watching.

A head emerges from the waters.

"Hi, Daphne," Onasander says, speaking softly.

The siren that had so terrified them back in the maze now looks bashful, tranquil. No longer the black-eyed, fang-toothed zombie intent on drowning them, but a dark-haired, rosy beauty.

"It's a good thing Onasander warned me about you," she

says, her voice tinkling, to Li'l Kimmy. "You pack a fiery punch."

Li'l Kimmy feels her stomach drop to her feet. She attacked this woman! This siren. This . . . well, who is she?

"I'm so sorry!" Li'l Kimmy says. "I didn't know you were . . ."

"A friend," Onasander finishes for her. "It's all right, Li'l Kimmy, Daphne knew what the test was all about. She agreed to it."

"I thought it would be fun to play a little prank on you all," Daphne says, her elbows on the rim of the lagoon and her chin in her palms. "But don't worry. Fire doesn't bother me."

"Now, Daphne, back to business," Onasander says. "I happen to remember that I gave you something to protect. Is that right?"

"You remembered! How?" Daphne purrs.

"Thanks to these four right here." Onasander points. "They figured out the puzzle."

"It was really Edwin," Julie says, pushing him forward a little.

Edwin blushes, his cheeks getting hot.

"Nicely done, Edwin." Daphne winks. "I'll go get it. One moment."

She disappears into the depths.

"What's down there?" Dilip says, leaning over the edge and staring with amazement.

"Careful, Dilip," Onasander says. "Don't fall in."

Daphne reemerges a few moments later with an oyster shell clasped between her hands.

"It's in here, in the pearls," she tells them. *Something undetectable hidden in something detectable.* "Be careful: As soon as you shuck the oyster, it'll all come out."

Onasander nods. "Thank you, Daphne. It's been lovely to see you. Thank you for protecting this."

She nods and blows kisses as they walk away. "Come back and let me know how it all turns out!"

Chapter Thirty-Seven

THE UNDETECTABLE

They return to the original lab, Onasander's study, and gather in the library, taking seats on the red leather couches. The oyster shell is in Onasander's lap. He gazes at it fearfully. How to protect it now? YAK has breached the Octagon Valley Institute, and it's only a matter of time before they find the main laboratory.

"Now, we have a choice to make, Octos," Onasander tells them, his face devoid of the glee or delight they've grown used to. He's as serious as he is on television. "I think, given everything you've done for me today, and everything we still have left to do together, you need to be a part of this decision."

Time for us to get serious too.

Onasander explains the choice that lies before them. Given that YAK has breached the Institute, there are only two ways to stop them from getting the Impossibilium. The first is to destroy the Impossibilium and therefore eradicate Impossibilium from the known universes, preventing YAK from ever getting their hands on any ever again.

"However," he warns, "Impossibilium is very powerful in beneficial ways as well as destructive ways. There is a lot of good that can be done with this substance. It has properties that are found nowhere else on this Earth, or in this reality. Destroying it would also mean destroying our chances of helping the world in those ways."

"Like what?" Julie asks.

"Some of my researchers and I believe that, given the tests we've been running, Impossibilium could be essential to solving the energy crisis on Earth." Onasander looks grieved. "There are so many world-bettering possibilities that it could be used for. But we can't keep it here in the Institute either. YAK will find it. They've stolen it from me before." He shudders. "And as I've explained, the results were . . . not good."

"What's the other choice?"

"We hide it again," says Onasander. "But not here. Somewhere else. Somewhere safer. Though where that could possibly be, I haven't a clue. We have more advanced security here than they have at the Pentagon."

"If only there was a way to take it someplace far, far away," says Li'l Kimmy.

"Hold on, I have an idea," Dilip says. "What if I take the Impossibilium and fly away with it?"

"They'll chase after you, Dilip," Onasander warns.

"I don't mind. Like you said, I'll be flying faster than seems possible. I'll just keep going and going; they'll never catch up with me!"

Dilip feels a rush of confidence as he thinks about it. He's been a C student his whole life. He never thought that his surfing or skateboarding was anything but a diversion. He never thought of himself as special, or talented, or able to contribute in any meaningful way. But after today, he feels like he can be useful, prove himself, succeed like his parents have always dreamed for him. This might be his chance to shine.

"So, what, you're just going to keep flying forever?" Julie asks. "That seems tiring. Even if you do have the power of flight."

"Not forever. Just . . . really far."

"Are you sure, Dilip?" Onasander asks.

"I'm sure. Completely."

"It's not a bad idea," Onasander says. "And with your jetpack, that could go quite well. But where would you fly it to?" He ponders for a moment. Then something strikes him. "I know just where to hide it!" he says excitedly.

"Where?!" Julie says, sitting up, thrilled.

"I can't tell you."

"What? Why?!" Li'l Kimmy says.

"No one can know. Well, except you, Dilip."

"No fair!" Li'l Kimmy crosses her arms.

"But he won't know for long. And neither will I. After you return, I'll have to give you a forgetfulness pass."

"How will we ever find it again?" Edwin inquires. "If we need it someday?"

"A good point, Edwin. I'll make another map, a pattern of clues of some kind that only I can read, so that eventually I'll be able to remember where it is."

"Just like with Daphne and the final puzzle piece," Julie notes. "Do you do this kind of thing often?"

"I have a lot of things to protect." Onasander shrugs. He taps his fingers against the sides of his forehead, thinking.

At last, he stands up, motions Dilip over, and whispers instructions in his ear. "You got that?"

Dilip looks, suddenly, like he might vomit.

"Can you handle it?" asks Onasander. "It's okay if you can't, but you must be sure."

Dilip swallows. He nods. He surfed the category-five hurricane waves off the Outer Banks last November. He can handle anything.

Onasander places the oyster shell in Dilip's palm. "Okay, then. Keep this safe. I heard that your board shorts have very secure pockets?"

The four of them smile, despite themselves.

Dilip feels a rush like he's never known. He is in possession of an unknown substance that has such intense power, it could save the world. Or, um, destroy it.

"Now, I have to arrange all the clues. You all hang tight. I'll be right back." With that, Onasander slips out the laboratory's door.

"And here I thought I was going to be sitting in a boring lecture all day," Li'l Kimmy says to the group, getting comfortable.

Chapter Thirty-Eight

EXTRA, EXTRA

Alas, the comfort is over too soon. The very moment the door disappears behind Onasander, a loud *CRACK* comes from the observatory window. Julie looks up, and Edwin watches her face quickly shift from calm to horror. "YAK!" she says, scrambling up.

"Not a great moment for Double O to leave us here!" Dilip says.

"Double O?" says Edwin.

"I'm trying it out," says Dilip.

There's another *crack* at the window. They can see the silvery figures beyond the glass. There are sparks and flames too. Are they using a *blowtorch*?

"What are we supposed to do, just wait for him to get

back?" Li'l Kimmy shouts. "They might have hacked their way through the roof by then!"

Edwin remembers the infinity-shaped object he swiped from Onasander's shelf of inventions. "This would really be a last resort, but I have an idea. . . ."

"Go on," says Julie.

Edwin clears his throat. "I could detonate this explosive," he offers, holding up the infinity symbol that's hovering over his palm.

It has swirling patterns ever shifting on its surface. Fiery red, smoky blue, sparkly gray.

"Detonate that? Is that a bomb?" Dilip says, brow furrowed.

"Not exactly. I don't like bombs. They're much too chaotic; you can never predict what they'll hit. Plus, I'm morally opposed to them."

"Okay, same, but what the heck is the difference between this and a bomb, then?" Li'l Kimmy asks, her tone of voice growing increasingly frantic. "I mean, what else do you detonate other than a bomb?"

"According to the small type on its face, it's a controlled explosive device. It only affects humans. So if we set it off in here, we should be totally fine."

"Fine?" Dilip exclaims. "Fine?! What do you mean fine?! We'll be killed!"

"No, Dilip, you didn't hear me properly. I said it only affects *humans!*" Edwin emphasizes.

Li'l Kimmy, Julie, and Dilip exchange looks as if they're worried for Edwin's sanity.

"You can't be serious," Edwin says, exasperated. "I mean, it's pretty obvious by now, isn't it? You haven't figured it out yet?"

All too true. Who's been waiting for this revelation for chapters and chapters? Raise your hand! Alas, our heroes are a bit behind.

"Figured *what* out, Edwin?" Li'l Kimmy exclaims.

"Yeah, what's obvious?" Dilip wants to know.

Edwin is wide-eyed—dumbfounded. He smiles and points at them with both hands.

"We're not human. We're aliens."

"What?!"

"Remember what the test is called? The Octagon Valley Assessment for the Extra-Ordinary. We're *Extra*! As in *extra-terrestrial*! All of us. You're an alien, you're an alien, you're an alien. And so am I! How is this a surprise?"

The three of them are speechless, although Julie is beginning to smirk. "I knew it. I knew you knew something."

"We have powers," Dilip says slowly. "*Extra* powers."

"Exactly." Edwin nods. "I can move things with my mind. And, Julie, you can control people's minds with your music. You can control *fish* minds with your music! Didn't you think that's a bit strange? Do you think every musically inclined middle schooler can do that?"

"No," Julie agrees with a smile. "At least, not many."

"And, Li'l Kimmy," Edwin goes on. "You can shoot fire from your *eyes*. You don't find *that* a bit strange and inhuman?"

"I thought maybe that was just something that happens in the Octo maze!" Li'l Kimmy explains.

"Dilip, you can straight-up fly! Like Superman! Superman was an alien, you know. He's from another planet. Just like us."

"Superman, huh?" Dilip likes the sound of that.

The implications of what Edwin is saying sink in slowly. They're from another planet? Then how are they here now?

"A lot of the stuff in this building is also alien," Edwin continues. "That's why it's so strange to us. It's technology we've never seen before, substances we never could have imagined, creatures out of a storybook. Remember what Maureen said? *Maybe it's not science from this Earth.* She might be evil, but she knew."

The Octo maze, the doors that lead to a million different rooms each time you open them, the technology, Daphne the siren, the strange plants.

"And this." Edwin holds up the swirling explosive. "This is alien too. Which means that it won't hurt us, or anything in the Institute. But it'll stop YAK."

"So we detonate it?" asks Julie.

"I don't think we have a choice," says Li'l Kimmy.

The sounds of the YAKs drilling their way in through the window is louder than ever. A deafening *crack* rings through the air. Green gloop shoots through the window's shattered glass.

YAK!

"But wait!" Julie says. "If we're aliens, doesn't that mean—"

But she doesn't have time to finish her sentence before the room explodes into darkness.

PART FOUR:
DEATH
TO
YAK!

Chapter Thirty-Nine

EVEN MORE EXTRA

At first, everything is still. The explosion has created something beyond perception. A sound so loud you can't hear it. A fire so hot you can't feel it. A moment so quick it seems to last forever.

Then the four Octos are thrown backward through the air from the force of the explosion. They land with a thud and a clatter as thousands of bottles and beakers and measuring cups topple around them to the floor.

The smoke from the explosion is a combination of the fiery red, smoky blue, and sparkly gray that was on the outside of the sphere. Edwin swipes at it, trying to clear enough to see his friends and rush to their sides. It seems like they're all unharmed, as he predicted. They're blinking, rubbing their eyes, checking their bodies to make sure they're still intact.

But then the smoke starts to settle, and glints of tinfoil silver send disco ball–like reflections around the room. Edwin gets a sinking feeling in his stomach.

Scattered across the room are YAKs. They look stunned, but they certainly don't look dead. Thank goodness for that. Violence is no solution!

The explosion only seems to slow them down. The YAKs are starting to wake up from their daze. They're getting up . . . and re-arming.

"Come on!" Edwin yells. "It's YAK!"

The word *YAK* rouses the three other Octos. They look around, taking in the smoky room, the bottles toppled to the floor, the library books strewn everywhere.

A familiar voice booms.

"What a joke!"

It's Maureen, brushing detritus from her skirt and standing by the spiral staircase. "A human-specific explosive. How sweet! You really thought that YAK is *human*?"

She screeches with laughter, and the YAKs start chuckling ugly little *yuck-yuck*s. Is *YAK* the sound they make?

"We're no more human than you are, Octos! We're probably even *less* human than you." She says it like that's a good thing, but Dilip has always liked humans. He never really knew there were other options. So far, though, the YAKs aren't giving the other options a great reputation.

"SHOOT!" she orders the YAKs. "GET THEM!"

Soon, the little tinfoil-clad creatures run toward the Octos, brandishing their weapons and shooting green gobs of goo everywhere.

"YUCK!" Li'l Kimmy is revolted.

"Don't you mean YAK?!" Julie corrects her.

Is that what YAK means? The green goop does sort of look like vomit. . . . Maybe it's vomit made from large hairy creatures commonly found in Tibet? No time to ponder as the four Octos dodge the green, slimy globs.

"UGH!" says Dilip, stepping into the goop. "Gross!"

"We can't get stuck!" says Edwin, dodging a large squirt of the stuff. "And we can't let them take the Impossibilium!"

Li'l Kimmy spots something that might help on the gadget spiral and grabs it. An umbrella! Perfect! Hopefully it's a special one! But isn't everything in this room special?

"Here!" she says, motioning for the rest of them to crowd underneath.

She lifts it up over their heads, then opens it. The umbrella fabric is printed with octagonal patterns, like a chic, designer umbrella.

Maureen peers over. "Wow, what a fabulous umbrella. But I really don't think it's going to help you losers."

One of the YAKs walks over to her.

"Uh, Maureen?" the YAK says.

"What?!" she screeches.

"That's not just an umbrella. I believe that's a force field."

"Oh. Well, can't you just shoot through it?" she asks the YAK.

The YAK shrugs.

"Shoot! Shoot!" she commands.

But the YAK is right. It *is* a force field! Once opened, the umbrella drops a shimmering substance that covers them, like a thin sheet that reaches to the ground.

Li'l Kimmy holds tightly to the umbrella as the YAKs, following Maureen's orders, shoot gloopy green slime toward them. It's an experience Li'l Kimmy could never have imagined. First of all, it rarely rains in LA, so she almost never uses an umbrella, let alone a magical alien (or whatever it is) force-field umbrella. And instead of protecting themselves from normal, earthly rain, they're protecting themselves from pulsing gobs of green goo being lobbed toward them.

The force field is doing a pretty good job keeping the gross, slimy Jell-O out, but with each gob that smacks against the force field, it shudders and thins slightly. Li'l Kimmy isn't sure how much longer it'll last. She never really thought too hard about how much she loves this reality. Now it's all she can think about.

Julie's head is spinning. Before coming to Octagon Valley's three-day summit, she had hoped, though she could barely admit to herself that she hoped it, that she'd make some friends she had something in common with. Standing with the Octos under an alien-umbrella force field with YAKs shooting gobs of potentially fatal green slime at them, she realizes that all her hopes have come true.

Just not in a way she could have ever predicted.

It's confusing, this idea that she's an alien. Are her parents still her parents? How did she come to Earth? Is she from a different planet, or a different reality? Are all the Octos from the same planet, or different ones? Each time they get a new answer, an exponential number of new questions seem to bloom.

Dilip, meanwhile, is itching to try out the jetpack. For once, he has talents that can be used for something more than his own amusement. He's always wondered how he was so naturally good at surfing and skating. Those moments when he felt himself rising, floating, like a great power was expanding within him—that was his alien self manifesting! He just had to let himself be joyful, vulnerable, and connected enough not to disregard it.

Li'l Kimmy has so many questions about her fire-shooting ability. How often can she do it? Are there drawbacks? Is the headset the only way to control it? Will she accidentally hurt one of her friends if she does it wrong? She does have to admit that it fits well with her personality. But wait, can aliens be rappers?

It's surprising to Edwin that it took the rest of the Octos this long to understand the fact that they're aliens. He'd expected that they'd sort of figured it out during the Octo maze when everyone started using their powers, but that they just didn't have enough time to talk about it.

He has always suspected he was different, that he is special, and yes, that he is Extra. When he got the letter, it was like being called home. He knew the Institute was where he belonged. As for his telekinetic ability? A bonus!

The YAKs keep shooting slime at their umbrella, which is holding for now.

"You guys, it's getting a little cramped in here," Li'l Kimmy notes.

"I don't think we'll be under here for much longer, even if we want to be," Edwin says grimly as the force field wavers.

"Edwin's right," Julie says. "We don't have much time. Dilip, you've got to get it out of here!"

"But what about you guys?" says Dilip.

"Don't look now," Li'l Kimmy says to the group, "but the force field is about to crack."

Chapter Forty

TEAMWORK MAKES THE DREAM WORK

It happens quickly. The force field flickers out, and the four of them are left standing under a normal, human umbrella. Li'l Kimmy tosses it to the side.

Her instincts are kicking in now. She knows that they're about to become green globs unless she does something. So Li'l Kimmy steps forward and launches the fire.

The other three Octos are in awe. Out of Li'l Kimmy's eyes, a ring of fire appears, surrounding the YAKs.

"Dilip, start flying!" she cries.

Dilip is pressing things on the jetpack, trying to figure out how to make it work. Meanwhile, green gloop is hitting the underside of Li'l Kimmy's fire. The green slime threatens to put out the fire, but she pushes on, holding tight.

It's exhausting, though, doing this. She feels her energy draining.

"Hurry up, Dilip, I don't know how much longer I can hold this!"

"But I don't know how to make this thing work!" Dilip says, struggling with the jetpack.

Suddenly, another door opens—and more familiar faces arrive!

From eons ago.

Or, okay, chapters.

It's Ting-Ting, Anton, and even Harold! Harold—what are you doing here?!

They rush over to the rest of the group.

"They're here!" says Anton, who isn't holding a game console!

"I told you!" says Ting-Ting, triumphantly holding up a brand-new notebook.

"I helped!" says Harold, who did no such thing but didn't want to be left in the dormitory alone.

(When the others left him at the beginning, he had to remain in that room for a very, very, very long time, as time works differently at the Institute. It would be nice to say that Harold used that time well, to contemplate his selfishness and decide to become a better person. Alas, he mostly cried until one of Onasander's researchers found him curled up in a fetal position, still clinging to his non-working phone.)

"Do you have it?" asks Anton, meaning the Impossibilium. It appears Onasander told them about it too. Wait—weren't they supposed to have their memories wiped?

"Yep," says Edwin.

"Then what are you waiting for? Get it out of here!" Anton yells.

"We're trying!" screams Julie.

"What are you guys doing here?" asks Edwin. "I thought you were done with this place!"

"Guess not," says Anton, looking embarrassed about his earlier actions.

"Dilip, try pressing the button in the middle of the right strap!" yells Ting-Ting, consulting her notes. "That should work!"

He presses it while she maneuvers a few different levers on his jetpack. There's a roaring sound, and the air grows warm around Dilip.

"That should do it," says Ting-Ting, stepping back.

"Okay," says Dilip. "See you soon, Octos," he adds, saluting.

Fabric extends out of the jetpack and surrounds Dilip's body. A suit manifests itself around his limbs and torso, while a helmet unfolds from the top of the pack and secures itself over his head.

"No time for big goodbyes!" Li'l Kimmy yells, eyes laser-focused on the YAKs.

Dilip lifts off the ground, using his own natural power

at first. Then he hits a lever and starts flying fast. But Li'l Kimmy loses steam. She collapses onto the ground, every drop of energy sapped. The wall of fire drops too, and suddenly, they're all defenseless. Including Dilip.

He's high enough that he's out of their reach—for now. Julie and Edwin make panicked eye contact. They need to do something! In a flash, Julie closes her eyes and starts concentrating.

She prays that her conducting works not only on animals, but on humans too. Or, wait, not humans, aliens. Are they aliens? Whatever the YAKs are, she hopes it works on them. She starts humming, her hands raised.

"Oh crud! Cover your ears, YAKs!" Maureen says, no longer using any niceties.

But it's too late. No green goo. The YAKs all have a calm expression on their faces as they sway back and forth. Even Maureen looks chilled out, for once.

"Go, Dilip, go!" Edwin cries.

Dilip, still working out the kinks with the jetpack, is hovering and looping around high above them. At last, he zooms out of the smashed window and toward goodness knows where.

At least the Impossibilium is safe, but they're still surrounded by YAKs with no more umbrella.

"We've got to get rid of them!" says Harold, wiping his forehead with his handkerchief. "I can't get slime on this cashmere sweater!"

"Look! A door!" Anton points. There is a door, but it's neither silver nor gold. It's a turgid, slimy green. Just like the green door that the YAKs first entered from.

"The door—it must be a portal to their home planet," says Edwin, his heart pumping fast. He's so excited, he forgets his anxiety or even to square-breathe. He's got this!

"If only we could open it!" says Ting-Ting. "But it's so far!"

Edwin thinks fast. "Julie, do you think you can keep this up for a few minutes longer?"

She nods, concentrating.

"Okay. I'm going to open that door with my mind. Julie, you make them all walk through it, all right?"

She nods again.

Edwin focuses on the green door, and from afar, they can see the doorknob turning left, then right, then left again.

It slams open!

An intense gravity overwhelms the room. The YAKs, at first, seem to resist its pull. But Julie instructs them to walk through. She conducts them toward the portal.

Maureen suddenly snaps out of her trance. "No! You morons!" she screams. "Keep shooting! Ignore her music! Nooooo! This is not fair! This is not fair!"

She shakes her fist as each and every YAK walks through the door and back to wherever they came from.

Harold shuts the door firmly behind them and frowns at Maureen, who's sobbing as she falls in a heap on the floor. "You look like you need to speak to the manager," he tells her.

"Cheer up. At least your hair still looks good," says Ting-Ting.

Anton grins. "That was pretty sick! We did it!"

Julie sits down gingerly, joining Li'l Kimmy on the ground. They both look exhausted. Edwin exhales, and it feels like the first real breath he's taken in a while.

The Impossibilium is safe out there with Dilip. YAK is defeated. But where on earth is Onasander?

Chapter Forty-One

COINKIDINKS

And so, our Octos finally, finally, get to rest. It's not quite a seminar, but at this point, they'd take dinner over a lecture in a heartbeat.

Wait, do aliens have hearts?

Another question for Onasander, who briefly reunited with our Octos just to escort Maureen to a quiet room where she could sob in peace.

"You know, I'm actually going to miss this freaky place," Dilip says, loading his plate with heaps of food. The Octos are finally eating. It's a midnight feast, and if they didn't have their alien metabolism to sustain them, they'd have been passed out long ago, as the only thing they've eaten all day is a snack bag of Hot Cheetos.

The dining hall is just a few quick silver doors and a few

knob turns away from the main lab. They sit all together at a long wooden table, passing around dishes that Onasander's kitchen researchers have made from plants and ingredients grown in the greenhouse. There's nothing like Li'l Kimmy's ever tasted. She can't stop eating this delicious salty dish that reminds her of congee but is lavender-colored.

"How is it that one day can feel like a whole lifetime?" Li'l Kimmy asks.

"How is it that an hour can feel like one second?" Julie jokes, elbowing Li'l Kimmy.

"True." Li'l Kimmy nods with her mouth full. "Our sense of time and space is totally messed up now."

"You're telling me. I have a whole chunk of my day erased from my memory!" Dilip says.

It's a strange feeling, not knowing where the past few hours have gone. He knows that he flew somewhere—the Octos and Onasander told him that—but he doesn't know where. They don't know, nor does Onasander. He had his own forgetfulness pass on the way back and went a bit too far with it; he never came back to the lab because he temporarily spaced on how to get there.

The other weird time warp they're all going through is how little time they have left with each other. They all sort of get along now.

Even with Harold.

"So, I fell asleep in that courtyard, and the next thing I knew I was waking up back in the library," says Ting-Ting.

"No idea how I got there. But Onasander was there, and he gave me a choice."

"He gave all of us the same choice," Anton says, reaching for a pastry that's a cross between a potato roll and a dumpling.

"He told us he could call our parents to pick us up, or we could stay and help," says Harold.

Dilip and Julie exchange a look. If Harold had the option to call his parents, then why on earth is he still here?

"I figured I'd stay, especially since my powers haven't manifested yet," Anton says with a shrug.

"My mom said I couldn't leave. Shocker," says Ting-Ting. "And Onasander says just because I didn't see the one hundred and eighth question doesn't necessarily mean I'm not an Octo. Especially since my mom figured out how to see it."

And Harold?

"Once my cell service worked, my dad didn't even pick up the phone. They're in the Maldives," explains Harold with a glum look on his face. "So I guess I'm stuck here, even if I'm human."

Aha! There you go. Something finally (finally!) makes sense.

After dinner, Onasander (finally recalibrated enough from the forgetfulness pass, which, in large doses, can really mess you up) joins them.

He takes a seat at the head of the table. After an hour

of nonstop chatter, the Octos are finally quiet, hoping for some answers.

Onasander takes a breath, crosses his legs, and rests his arms on the armrests of his rather throne-like chair.

"Let me get one thing out of the way," he begins. "My approach to introducing you all to your Octo lives as aliens was, shall we say, certainly less than ideal."

The Octos try not to smirk and laugh, but they notice how somber Onasander is. Almost like the Onasander they've seen on TV.

"But you should know, I've never done this before. Not that that is exactly an excuse."

He sighs, putting a hand to his forehead briefly and closing his eyes. He regains composure and goes on.

"Initially, I had hoped to just put you through a series of tests in order to see if you are capable of handling this ultrasensitive information. After I had confirmed this, my plan was to gently reveal your alien nature to you throughout the three-day summit's lectures to soften the shock of being told the truth about yourselves. I hoped to expand your minds so much during the three-day summit that by the time you were let in on the secret, you would take it eagerly and with open minds."

The Octos all nod. That seems pretty ideal. Would've been nice.

"What I did not count on, however, was a battle with

YAK and an unceremonious dropping of truth bombs. But all's well that ends well, now that YAK was sent back to their home planet. I am a pacifist, after all. I believe that everyone has their rightful place in the universe. But YAK's rightful place is far, far away from here."

"What is YAK, anyway?" asks Julie, who still wants to know. "What does it stand for?"

"Good question," says Onasander. "But one I can't answer. You'll have to ask them the next time we see them. Hopefully, that won't be for a while."

"You don't know?" Li'l Kimmy is floored.

"They've never actually said." Onasander tilts his head, looking up at the ceiling, as if the answer will present itself. "But whatever it means, they're the reason you're all here. I came up with the Octagon Valley Assessment for the Extra-Ordinary because my multiverse-activity sensors detected YAK moving toward our reality. I knew they'd found me again and were after the Impossibilium. I needed help. You see, I came here to this planet about twelve years ago, and I've known all along that there were others like me. Unfortunately, the others were a bit too embryonic for me to contact at the time."

"Twelve years ago? But that was when—" Julie calculates in her mind.

"You were all born, yes. Except for Edwin. He's younger, since his alien father was already building a life here."

A burst of emotion thrums in Edwin's chest. *Alien father?*

"Okay, but how did we get here? Where did we come from?" asks Edwin.

So like Edwin to be asking the sensible questions, even when a huge truth bomb is dropped.

"Well, as I mentioned earlier, when YAK tried to create the one hundred and nineteenth element, they destroyed a reality," Onasander explains. "This act of destruction sent alien matter all over the universe. Life finds a way, you see. You Octos are all that remains of that reality. You and I are from the reality that was destroyed."

"We are?" asks Julie, a swelling in her chest.

"Yes, all of you, except maybe for Harold."

Oh, Harold!

"But, you know, he might be an Octo still. He did pass the Assessment, after all. No matter *how* he did it, he did do it," Onasander muses.

Edwin, Julie, Li'l Kimmy, Dilip, Ting-Ting, Anton, and Harold are all silent as they take this in. They're aliens from another reality, a reality that was annihilated by YAK. The thought subdues them all.

Yes, even Harold.

"Onasander, I have one last question," says Edwin.

"What's that, my boy?"

"Is there any ice cream in this place?"

The group instantly perks up.

They scream! Yes! Ice cream!

And that's what makes Edwin a good leader.

"So I'm starting a group chat for us, yeah?" Li'l Kimmy says, pulling out her phone once she's fully stuffed with rocky road and caramel sauce. "Everyone put in your number and pick your emojis."

Julie takes the phone and chooses the violin and the ghost as her emojis. Anton chooses a sheep. Edwin, an infinity symbol. Harold, the dollar sign. Ting-Ting, a notebook.

Onasander has told them that given the overwhelming nature of the day, the Octos should take some time to go back to their normal lives and try to process what went on this weekend. He worries that he's dropped the information on them too quickly. They're all invited to come back and spend the entire summer at Octagon Valley, when Onasander will reveal more about their alien nature. But for now, they're to say goodbye.

Edwin is disappointed. There's not much about his normal life he wants to go back to, other than his mom. He gets the sense that the other Octos feel the same way.

"Why do we have to all live so far apart?" Dilip gripes as he types in the surfer and the dove emoji. "We live all the way across the country from each other!"

"I know, it's like, now we don't get to hang out again until the summer?" Li'l Kimmy says. "That blows!"

"That may very well be the case," says Onasander as the ice cream detritus is cleared away. "But nevertheless, your parents will be here tomorrow afternoon to pick you up. I've already contacted them."

"They're coming *early*?" asks Ting-Ting. "Even *my* mother?"

"Even your mother, Ting-Ting," says Onasander with a kind smile.

At that moment, one of Onasander's research assistants runs into the room. He bends sideways slightly so she can whisper into his ear, and Onasander's face grows slack and stricken. He nods, whispers something back to the assistant, and takes a deep breath.

"Is something wrong?" Edwin asks. *Do we get to stay?* he adds silently.

"Octos," Onasander says in a grave voice. "Unfortunately, I don't think I'll be able to send you home tomorrow after all."

The Octos grab each other's hands in delight. They're not going home yet?! A thrill runs up their spines. But then, why doesn't Onasander seem happy about this?

There's a loud rumble, and the ground shakes once more.

YAK?

Nope!

Onasander sighs. "It appears Maureen has escaped with the moon rocket—that rumble would be her taking off— and we're going to have to go after her. You see, um, her dads will not be happy if they can't pick her up on Monday. Or if they have to pick her up in pieces." He chuckles nervously. "So, alas, it appears we have some work to do. In space. The thing is, I do need all eight of you for something special. Even Maureen."

Oh ho ho ho! Eight kids. Eight sides to an octagon. Not a coinkidink after all!

It never is!

BWHAHAHAHAHA!

Now you know what an unreliable narrator is—but never fear. BOOK TWO is on its way! And that, you can count on!

Acknowledgments

An infinity-sized thanks to my dear editor Kieran Viola, who has the same sense of humor as I do and got this book immediately and made it so much better! As well as to my awesome team at the MDLC Studio at Disney: Brittany Rubiano, Augusta Harris, Candice Snow, Rachel Stark, Crystal McCoy, Matt Schweitzer, Holly Nagel, and Ann Day. You guys rock!!! Thank you for everything!

Octos wouldn't be around without my stalwart supporters at 3Arts, Richard Abate and Hannah Carrende. Thanks also to my TV/film mama, the great EGV (Ellen Goldsmith-Vein), and her team at Gotham Group: Jeremy Bell, DJ Goldberg, and Sarah Jones. Love you all!

Thanks to all my friends and family and my wonderful readers for hanging around for all the rides.

FALL INTO THE RABBIT HOLE

with this latest installment in the *New York Times* best-selling Descendants series

ON SALE
5.7.24